Praise for *The Reader on the 6.27*

'Charming . . . It is a clever, funny and humane work that champions the power of literature'   *Sunday Times*

'A delightful tale . . . Much of the charm resides in the simplicity of Didierlaurent's prose and his vivid characterization. Ros Schwartz's translation perfectly conveys the warmth and eccentricities of his memorable cast. Already a bestseller in France, *The Reader on the 6.27* looks set to woo British readers and become a book club favourite'   *Independent on Sunday*

'I read it in one sitting, I couldn't put it down! It is one of those feel-good books that gets you really invested in the character's story, and then puts you in a good mood when you finish it'   *Hello!*

'The humanity of the characters . . . the re-enchantment of everyday life, the power of words and literature, tenderness and humour . . . *The Reader on the 6.27* is a must'   *L'Express*

'A beautiful testimony to the universality of the love of books'   *Livres Hebdo*

'This enchanting story is a valuable discovery'   *Télé 7 Jours*

'A pleasing fable about the power of literature to elevate our lives'   *Birmingham Post*

THE REST OF THEIR LIVES

JEAN-PAUL DIDIERLAURENT won a number of short-story competitions and was twice awarded the Hemingway Prize before the resounding success of his first novel, the bestselling *The Reader on the 6.27*, which has been published in over thirty countries. *The Rest of their Lives* is his second novel.

Also by Jean-Paul Didierlaurent

THE READER ON THE 6.27

JEAN-PAUL DIDIERLAURENT

THE REST OF THEIR LIVES

Translated by Ros Schwartz

PAN BOOKS

First published 2017 by Mantle

This paperback edition published 2018 by Pan Books
an imprint of Pan Macmillan
20 New Wharf Road, London N1 9RR
Associated companies throughout the world
www.panmacmillan.com

ISBN 978-1-5098-4036-6

Originally published in French 2016 as *Le reste de leur vie* by Au diable vauvert

The right of Jean-Paul Didierlaurent to be identified as the
author of this work has been asserted by him in accordance
with the Copyright, Designs and Patents Act 1988.

9 8 7 6 5 4 3 2 1

A CIP catalogue record for this book is available from the British Library.

Typeset by Palimpsest Book Production Limited, Falkirk, Stirlingshire
Printed and bound by CPI Group (UK) Ltd, Croydon, CR0 4YY

Visit **www.panmacmillan.com** to read more about all our books
and to buy them. You will also find features, author interviews and
news of any author events, and you can sign up for e-newsletters
so that you're always first to hear about our new releases.

To Sabine, Marine and Bastien,
my three suns.

To my mother,
for the life lesson that she
gives us every day.

1

Manelle was on edge, as she always was when she crossed the threshold of Marcel Mauvinier's apartment. This man had the art of driving her round the bend. 'You won't forget to empty my pot, will you, mademoiselle?' was his usual greeting. Never hello, or the least word of welcome. No, just this call to order barked from the living room where his posterior was glued to an armchair from dawn till dusk: 'You won't forget to empty my pot, mademoiselle?' Implying that she was in the habit of not emptying his wretched pot. But that was the only thing Manelle thought about when she came here, the enamel chamber pot painted with purple flowers which she had to lug every morning from the bedroom to the bathroom to pour the contents – the product of a night of prostate disorder – down the toilet.

At almost eighty-three, having recently lost his wife, Mauvinier was entitled to four hours of home care a week, spread over five forty-eight-minute visits from Monday to Friday. Visits during which, as well as emptying the old boy's chamber pot, Manelle had to carry out a number of chores including vacuuming, making the bed, doing the ironing and peeling vegetables, all under the wary eye of the old monster who always tried to get more than his money's worth. 'I've made a list for you,' he simpered. Every morning she found the sheet of squared paper with a list of the day's tasks lying on the waxed kitchen tablecloth. Manelle slipped on her pale green overalls and scanned Marcel Mauvinier's cramped handwriting, the writing of a skinflint which never strayed outside the lines. Words written parsimoniously.

> Empty chamber pot
> Hang out washing
> Put a white wash on
> Make the bed (change the pillowcase)

Water the *ficus* in the dining room

Sweep kitchen + passage

Go down and fetch post

Marcel Mauvinier, former owner of a domestic appliance store, had become a champion at the little game of how-to-keep-your-home-help-busy-for-forty-eight-minutes. Manelle always wondered why they were called home helps – skivvies would be more apt. She checked her instructions again, trying to guess where the old ogre could have hidden the fifty-euro note today. She was ready to bet on the *ficus*. The money had become Manelle's daily quest. Finding its hiding place was a challenge that spiced up the forty-eight minutes ahead. A year earlier, when for the first time she had come across the banknote that seemed to have been innocently left on the bedside table, she had stopped in mid-air as she was about to pick it up. The words 'danger' and 'minefield' had flashed across her mind. This highly visible fifty-euro note, lying nice and flat in the middle of the little doily on the bed-side table, had felt a bit too obviously like a trap to be genuine. Marcel Mauvinier was not the sort to leave money lying around, let alone a large amount. For a few seconds, Manelle thought of all the things she could do with such a sum. Meals out, cinema, clothes, books and shoes had danced in front of her eyes. Things as specific as that pair of funky sandals she'd spotted the previous day in the window of San Marina on sale at €49.99 briefly entered her head. In the end, she decided to ignore the money. She made the bed and left the room without a glance at the lace-framed fifty-euro note taunting her.

Marcel Mauvinier had torn himself away from his TV screen to point his nose in the direction of the kitchen.

'Is everything all right?' the old man had inquired as she was filling in the time sheet. Never until now had the old man shown any concern for her wellbeing.

'Yes, everything's fine,' she replied, looking him in the eye.

'No problems?' he added suspiciously, padding towards the bedroom.

'Ought there to be a problem?' she'd asked innocently behind his back.

The sight of his discombobulated expression on his return to the kitchen had delighted Manelle. A discomfiture that in her eyes was worth a lot more than fifty miserable euros.

Ever since that day, the note numbered U18190-

763573 – Manelle had jotted down the number to check whether it was always the same one – had travelled to the four corners of Marcel Mauvinier's apartment. Tantalizing Manelle seemed to have become one of the old man's reasons for living. The CCTV cameras had appeared a little later. A whole network of miniature cameras carefully positioned so as to cover almost the entire 110 square metres. Manelle had counted five. One in the kitchen, one in the bedroom, one covering the passage, one in the bathroom and another in the living room. Five cold black eyes that recorded her every movement. But the octogenarian had fallen into his own insidious trap by creating an idiotic addiction that consisted of trying to catch his home help stealing from him red-handed. One day she'd surprised the old ogre when he was watching the previous day's footage. The minute she had the chance, Manelle had blinded the miniature cyclops by moving an object so it obscured the view, or given a vigorous flick of the duster, re-angling the camera towards the floor or the ceiling. Not once had Manelle mentioned the nomadic banknote, something that continued to puzzle Mauvinier and irritate him greatly. Several times, the young woman had been tempted to turn the note over, or fold it in four, just to signal to this crazy old man that she wasn't fooled by his little game, but in the end she decided that to ignore the fifty euros completely was the best way of paying her tormentor back. So, every day, the bank-note lay waiting for her. On the rug in the living room, on top of the washing machine, on the fridge, wedged between two books, next to the telephone, in the shoe closet, on top of a pile of towels in the bathroom cup-board, in the fruit basket, slipped in among a pile of letters. Or, like today, under the *ficus* to be watered. The note was poking out from beneath the terracotta pot. As she was fetching the post from the letter box downstairs, Manelle suddenly wondered anxiously how she would react if one day Marcel Mauvinier were to tire of the game and put the note back in his wallet once and for all. She had ended up growing fond of the fifty-euro note that turned her round of chores into a treasure hunt.

At 9.45 precisely, once her work was done, Manelle removed her overalls and signed the time sheet. From having seen him do so time and time again, she knew that at the same time Marcel Mauvinier was fishing out the pocket watch he kept hidden in his waistcoat to check that she had scrupulously adhered to the allotted forty-eight minutes.

2

Every morning, as soon as he had eaten the three buttered crispbreads spread with blackberry jam – the only kind he liked – and taken a few sips of *café au lait*, Ambroise hastily put the bowl and breakfast things in the sink, wiped away the crumbs scattered over the wax cloth, then crept down the long corridor that ran the length of the apartment. He never failed to stop halfway, by the first door, and press his ear to the wooden panel that barely dampened Beth's snores. He loved listening to the deep glottal noises that emanated from the elderly woman. Today, from the depths of the room, the sound of a becalmed sea reached his ears, the waves washing over the shingle followed by the fizzing of the sand. Inhalation, exhalation. Ebb and flow. Reassured, Ambroise continued down the corridor and slipped noiselessly into the bathroom adjacent to his room. The tired neon strip light always flickered twice before bathing the floor and walls in its cold light. A rectangle of plywood covered the ancient hip bath cluttering the space. Ambroise was always filled with the same sense of wonderment on seeing the makeshift draining board where the instruments lay. Spread out on the terry towel that had absorbed their moisture during the night, they gleamed brightly under the harsh lighting. He never tired of gazing at the sparkling reflections of the stainless-steel surfaces. That moment suspended in time when he found himself alone with them in the tiny, overheated room smelling of detergent gave him a particular thrill. He quietly ran through his checklist, his eyes darting from right to left over the terry towel. Scalpel, aneurysm hooks, bone separators, fixation forceps, gathering forceps, straight scissors, curved scissors, curved and double-curved needles, probes, nose clamp, haemostatic forceps, incision spreaders, flexible and rigid spatulas. He picked up the instrument he found the most beautiful of them all, the trocar. The fifty-centimetre metal shaft was agreeable to the touch. Its point, sharpened like a pencil, had a dozen tiny holes which he carefully cleaned with a miniature brush. On the floor by the bath stood a bulky leather case with its flaps wide open, exposing its dark innards. Ambroise grabbed the shammy cloth hanging above the wash-basin and polished the instruments one by one to remove any last traces of moisture. The cloth glided along the needles, caressed the blades and made the handles gleam. One by one, he replaced the tools in their cases and put them away in the bag. After tossing the towel into the laundry basket, Ambroise closed and locked the case and took it into his room, where it joined its twin, an identical case which contained the pump and the embalming fluid. His mobile phone on the bedside table was vibrating frantically. Ambroise cleared his throat and took the call.

Roland Bourdin of Roland Bourdin & Sons never bothered to announce himself when he called, identi-fiable solely from the cold, distant tone he had always used with Ambroise. Over the four years that the young man had been working for the company, their relationship had not changed one jot. Professional and nothing more. With craggy features, a sickly pallor and a sparse goatee beard surrounding lips so thin that they were like blueish-purple scars, his boss was one of those people who look the way they sound. Since Monsieur Bourdin's only descendant was a daughter, the addition of '& Sons' to his company name had no other *raison d'être* than that of conferring on the firm a veneer of intergenerational respectability which reassured the clientele. Ambroise's boss was calling to book in a home visit. As was his wont, and with no linguistic flourishes other than what was strictly necessary for making himself understood, Bourdin rapped out the information in an order determined by him alone and from which he never departed: client's surname, first name, gender, age and address where the procedure was to take place. 'Didn't write down house number but it's yellow according to the wife,' he added curtly before hanging up. As sparing with his definite articles as he was with social niceties, thought Ambroise as he noted the details on his iPhone. He went into the vast main bathroom he shared with Beth, brushed his teeth, shaved, tamed his thick black mop with hair gel and spritzed his cheeks with two squirts of aftershave. On the hanger in the wardrobe, his work suit awaited him. White shirt, dark grey tie, black jacket and trousers. He eased his seventy-six kilos into the freshly ironed clothes. Later, he would don the protective clothing that was his real work outfit, the one people never saw, over the first, like a second skin. For now, appearances were paramount. Don't cause alarm, be as smooth as possible. A ghost, that's what he must try to be like. A ghost in a suit and tie who must leave no more trace than a passing shadow. Satisfied with his reflection in the mirror above the washbasin, Ambroise headed for the front door, swinging one precious case from each hand. A tourist setting off for a distant country, he thought with a smile. His grin broadened on seeing Beth standing in the middle of the corridor. Whatever the hour and despite all the precautions he took to be as discreet as possible, he always found the old lady barring his path when he left the apartment, offering him her radiant face. He bent his one-metre-eighty frame so that his grandmother could deposit the day's kiss on his forehead and whisper in his ear the word, 'Go,' which sounded like a blessing each time. More would have been pointless. That one syllable contained all the love in the world.

3

'At the roundabout, take the third exit then keep right,' boomed Fabrice Luchini's rich thespian voice, filling the cab of the brand-new van and startling Ambroise. He hadn't yet got used to his GPS. 'This amazing technology gives you a whole array of famous voices to choose from,' the Renault salesman had told him when he went to pick up the vehicle. 'From Carole Bouquet to Jean Gabin, or Louis de Funès, Bourvil, Mitterrand, De Gaulle, Brigitte Bardot and lots of others,' the vendor had added proudly. Imagining De Gaulle suggesting he turn left or Mitterrand telling him to keep right amused Ambroise. He promised himself he would ditch Luchini at the first opportunity and replace him with Carole Bouquet. Once again, Bourdin had chosen white for this new acquisition. 'You are artisans like any others,' he dinned into his staff all year round. 'Artisans of the human body, fair enough, but you are still artisans. And artisans always drive white vans!' Ambroise was not particularly happy about turning up at clients' homes in the same sort of vehicle as a decorator, plumber or electrician. He would have preferred a nobler colour – the same grey, for example, as the one his boss kept for ceremonial hearses, a halfway colour that exuded neutrality, sobriety and efficiency. Instead, he had to be content with this non-colour, and all because Monsieur Bourdin wanted to save four hundred euros on the metallic paint option.

Fabrice broke in again. 'In two hundred metres, turn right, then you have reached your destination.' Rows of identical houses stood on either side of Impasse des Sorbiers. Dubiously Ambroise contemplated the dozens of small, cloned houses, all with the same garage and tiny conservatory, identical balconies and anthracite-grey slate roofs, the same dormer windows, each house enclosed by a conifer hedge. To his dismay, all the houses were painted some shade of yellow: straw, sunshine, lemon, canary, corn, broom, mustard. 'Thank you, Roland Bourdin & Sons,' he cursed under his breath. Trusting his instinct, he headed for the one which had the most cars standing outside. After parking his van half on the pavement with the rear parking sensors beeping tyrannically, he unloaded his two bulging bags and mounted the front steps. Before he could press the bell, the door opened to reveal a woman in her sixties with a puffy face, her eyes red from crying. Her whispered 'hello' barely passed the barrier of her lips. She was distracted, stumbled over her words, murmured rather than spoke. Like all the others, thought Ambroise. Grief had that terrible effect of muffling the vocal cords and stifling sounds in the back of the throat. He bowed his head in greeting to the small gathering in the house. People stood aside to make way for him as he followed the mistress of the house. The sadness imprisoned in the walls made the atmosphere suffocating. Ambroise took the woman and children to one side and explained very briefly why he was there, without really going into detail. Only give a vague idea, don't disclose anything of the process, that was the rule, whatever questions people asked. The less they knew, the better it was for all concerned.

He chose his words carefully, words tested on many occasions, words to soothe. He asked for access to a washbasin before being shown into the room. He reassured the woman one last time before entering. An hour and a half alone with her husband was all he required to do what had to be done.

4

The curtains had been drawn and the room was in half-darkness. The characteristic cloying smell that sometimes assailed his nostrils when he arrived in a home was imperceptible here. Ambroise put his bags down on the floor, turned on the centre light and opened the curtains to let in as much daylight as possible. On a chair, suit, shirt, tie and underwear had been neatly arranged, and on the floor was a pair of freshly polished shoes. The body lay on the bed. Sixty-something, very stout. Over ninety kilos, guessed Ambroise at a glance, pulling a face. This was going to take a toll on his back, once again. The man looked as though he'd enjoyed the good life. Ambroise was going to have to watch out. He had often been struck by how those who'd lived a good life made bad corpses. The gaping pyjama jacket revealed dark blotches on the man's sides. His ears and hands had already turned a lovely blueish purple. Ambroise removed his jacket, slipped on his white coat and a pair of latex gloves, and put a mask over his nose and mouth. He unfurled the plastic body bag next to the deceased and rolled the body onto it. Rigor mortis had already set in, making the limbs and jaws stiff. Relaxing the muscles was the first task. Ambroise grabbed one of the arms and moved it back and forth from the shoulder, then leaned on it with all his weight to bend the elbow. He took the hand and stretched and loosened the fingers. He did the same with the other arm, then attacked the legs. All this time, he was listening to the body, his gaze roving over the surface, attentive to the slightest detail. Cardiac massage, he inferred, noting the blueish area around the sternum. He manipulated the lower jaw to restore its mobility. Then Ambroise tackled the deceased head-on to raise him up and remove his pyjama top. 'Last tango, old fellow,' his former supervisor used to say to the person in his embrace. He had taught Ambroise everything he knew and was affectionately nicknamed the Master in the funeral business. 'Illusionists, Ambroise, that's all we are,' he would say. 'No more than illusionists whose job is to make people believe that everything stops the instant death strikes. Nonsense. Life doesn't stop with death, quite the opposite. It loves bodies, it's never finished with them. Without us, it would transform every corpse into an abomination. We're there to inhibit its invasive presence and repel it as if it were an army on the march. Hunt it down, deep inside the tiniest organs, then expel it and bolt the doors to defer the inevitable disintegration of the flesh. Magicians, young Padawan,' he would blaze proudly, 'that's what we are, magicians whose arduous task it is to transform corpses into peaceful slumberers.'

Once he had completely undressed the deceased, Ambroise opened the case containing the aspirator pump, pouches and collection jars. He filled the tank with water and prepared the embalming fluid by adding the formaldehyde-based preservative. The liquid was a lovely candy pink. He placed the electric pump on the bed and wedged the drip solution and collection bottles between the dead man's legs. He exhumed the instruments from the case and placed them on the stainless-steel tray, cut two lengths of ligature wire, connected the needle to the tube, prepared cotton-wool pads and took out two transparent eye patches. Ambroise loved these preliminaries. People must never see the equipment. It was a golden rule, as they must never be present during the process. The world of the living had no place here while he was at work. His former master was right. He was a magician and, like all magicians, he must not give away his secrets. Using a cotton-wool pad soaked in a moisturizing alcohol-based solution, he set about cleaning the nose and eyes and then placed the eye patches over the eyelids to keep the eyes closed. He spread massage cream over the deceased's face and ears. With a scalpel, Ambroise made an incision a few centimetres long at the base of the neck to extricate the artery, taking good care not to damage the neighbouring jugular vein full of blood. Once he had inserted the cannula into the artery and clamped it in place, he plugged in the electric pump which hummed gently and began injecting. Soon the veins swelled once more. He diligently massaged the hands, cheeks and ears to help the fluid penetrate. Still armed with his scalpel, Ambroise made a second, tiny incision between the navel and the sternum, through which he inserted the end of the aspirator tube. After injecting two litres of embalming fluid into the body, Ambroise punctured the heart with the trocar using a firm, precise movement. The blood spurted into the collecting pouch in a thick stream. He injected a second dose of fluid. Once again, the miracle occurred, as splendid as a sunrise pushing back the night. The blotches faded, the skin regained a pink hue, the cyanosis of the cheeks was dispelled as if by wizardry as the formaldehyde replaced the blood. The face, until now tense in death, softened and took on an appearance of serenity. Comforted to find himself sheltered from time, thought Ambroise. Still using the aspirator tube, Ambroise probed each organ in turn to collect the excess blood, urine and gas. Kidneys, lungs, bladder and stomach – with experience, the young embalmer knew exactly which organ he was in, depending on the density he encountered as he punctured the wall. Ambroise stopped the pump. Silence always caught him off guard. He smiled behind his mask. A deathly silence. He closed up the nostrils and throat by inserting wads of cotton wool deep inside then practising a mandibular suture with the curved needle. Less than one minute later, the invisible stitches between the lower jaw, the palate and the nasal septum held the jaws together. 'Another one who won't say a word,' the Master was in the habit of saying as he made each mouth suture. Ambroise removed the cannula and sutured the entry point. He took the bottle containing the cavity fluid, connected it to the trocar tube and raised the bottle above his head. Governed solely by the law of gravity, the liquid drained into the body and spread deep into the internal organs. Once the half-litre of embalming fluid was dispersed in the innards, Ambroise withdrew the draining tube, which he wiped thoroughly, then plugged the incision. The gestures of a mechanic after changing the oil in a car engine, he thought.

Ambroise delicately shaved the deceased's cheeks and chin. He washed the body with a cloth soaked in disinfectant, dried it, then began a new *pas de deux* to get the man's clothes on. For almost ten minutes, Ambroise manipulated his ninety kilos, puffing and panting, raising him up and rolling him over. He tied his shoelaces, buttoned up the jacket, adjusted his tie as best he could, then brushed his hair. Like an artist contemplating his work, he stepped back and, after giving it a final once-over, lightly dabbed the right ear, which was darker than the other, with a discreet layer of foundation. He adjusted the shirt collar, ensured the tie knot was in the centre and smoothed out a crease in the jacket. While the embalming techniques would always be invisible, the physical appearance is only the tip of the iceberg and it was vital to ensure that no detail, not even the most trivial, jeopardized the entire edifice. The body bag was folded underneath the corpse, on either side. The funeral parlour staff would be using it to transfer the body to the coffin. He pulled the bedspread up to the navel. Ambroise crossed the dead man's arms over his chest then inserted between his fingers the sprig of lily of the valley that was by the bed. He put his instruments away in the cases, the empty bottles, the pouches containing the bodily fluids and the bag of waste into which he dropped his mask and gloves. He swapped his overalls for his jacket, and one hour and twenty minutes after entering the bedroom, Ambroise emerged to invite the family to view the body. The verdict came from the mouth of the eldest daughter. 'My papa's so handsome,' she exclaimed, bathing the deceased's forehead in tears as she kissed him. Once again, the magic had worked. The embalmer took his leave as discreetly as he could, leaving no more trace or reminders of his passage than a ghost. A ghost whose telephone was vibrating in his pocket to inform him of his next assignment.

5

Samuel Dinsky was a breath of fresh air in Manelle's round. His eyes, two black marbles twinkling with mischief, would light up at the sight of the young woman. Always smiling, over the months Samuel had become much more than just a client. Eighty-two years old, slightly raised cholesterol, unmarried and with no family, the man was one metre sixty-five of cheeriness who hailed Manelle each day with genuine delight. Unlike others, the old man never spoke of the past. Perhaps the number tattooed in purple ink glimpsed one day on the inside of his forearm explained why. She was his Tinker Bell, his turtle dove, his rod and staff, his Cinderella, his sugar plum, his little poppy, his ray of sunshine, his sweetheart – he always had a fancy greeting for her when she arrived each morning. There was no ulterior motive behind the attention he lavished on her and there were no smutty innuendos beneath his words of endearment. Contrary to some old lechers with wandering hands who had an annoying tendency to confuse home help with call girl, Samuel expressed nothing other through these affectionate nicknames than his joy at seeing her between eleven and twelve every day, from Monday to Friday. She liked to think that this privilege was for her and her alone, even if a little voice inside her whispered that he was bound to behave in the same way with her colleagues and that these endearments were probably the best ploy he'd found to avoid muddling up their names. Samuel's small home in Rue d'Alger was just like its owner, simple and welcoming, with no unnecessary embellishments but not devoid of charm. Manelle loved working there. That hour with the old man had the same feel-good effect on her as sunbathing for the first time in early spring. She knocked discreetly on the door and went straight in.

'It's me,' she shouted from the hallway.

'How's my little angel this morning?'

'Your little angel's fine, thank you. And how are you?' she asked, depositing a kiss on each of the old man's rough cheeks, contravening one of the basic rules of the profession which was that all physical contact of an affectionate nature with the client was forbidden. Home help Mademoiselle Manelle Flandin must at all times confine herself to carrying out the official duties for which she was paid, no more and no less – duties which consisted of:

Washing the dishes

Doing the laundry

Hanging out the washing

Cleaning the windows

Ironing

Making the bed

Helping the client out of bed

Helping the client into bed

Help with personal hygiene

Help with dressing

Help with undressing

Shopping

Cooking meals

Feeding pets

Putting out the rubbish

Walking the dog

Sweeping and mopping the floors

Polishing wooden floors

Vacuuming

Closing or opening the shutters

Watering plants

and emptying Marcel Mauvinier's chamber pot.

It was in no way part of the home help's job to:

Read aloud every evening extracts from the latest bestseller to Annie Vaucquelin at bedtime to help her fall asleep

Manage Pierre Ancelin's share account

Spend an hour sorting out the Perron family photos

Have a coffee and a chat

Eat a slice of tart or cake over a chat

Watch and describe what's going on in *The Young and the Restless* with Jeannine Poirier who can no longer see

Play Scrabble with Ghislaine de Montfaucon

Mix a Negroni (one part Campari, one part vermouth, one part gin) for the widowed Madame Dierstein and raise a glass with her every Friday evening

Deposit kisses on Samuel Dinsky's rough cheeks every morning.

But Manelle didn't give a toss about the rules and no one could ever stop her kissing all the Samuel Dinskys on the planet by claiming that such tokens of affection were strictly forbidden by the home helps' bible.

'I'm always fine when I see my little domestic goddess.'

The packet of painkillers on the sideboard belied his words. For some time, the old man had been suffering from recurrent headaches, migraines that made his life a misery, sometimes for days on end. Recently, Manelle had caught an expression of pain distorting his features when he thought no one could see him. She counted the number of tablets missing from the packet and was worried.

'You've taken six since yesterday? That's a lot, you know. You spoke to the doctor yesterday afternoon, what did he say?'

'That despite my age, I had the blood pressure of a young man. He just renewed the prescription for my cholesterol pills and prescribed stronger painkillers, but I'm finishing these first.'

'And that's all?'

'No, I've got to have an MRI in two weeks and maybe see a neurologist or whatever. What's for lunch today, beauty?'

Even though he still cooked occasionally, Samuel had requested meals on wheels. Reading the day's menu was Manelle's first job on arriving at his home. A ritual she threw herself into with gusto, putting on a feigned solemnity, she would grab the card with the week's gourmet offerings in copperplate handwriting. Manelle climbed onto a chair and, like a town crier, declaimed the dishes in a clear, sing-song voice, under the amused gaze of Samuel who was in seventh heaven.

'And this Tuesday the twelfth of April we will have a starter of mortadella on a bed of baby leaves, followed by chicken breast garnished with Peter-the-Great-style potato and celeriac mash. And for dessert, the chef proposes a dairy whip with a fruits-of-the-forest coulis. Master chef Queux thanks you for any feedback that will help him improve the quality of the service, except perhaps being told that these vegetable dishes with mouth-watering names like puréed broad beans, Conti lentils, Crécy carrots or Peter-the-Great-style celeriac like today, once they are served up, all end up looking like a heap of steaming poo-green dung from the same orifice!'

Samuel applauded Manelle's performance vigorously. She spent the following fifty minutes bustling around, dashing from the bedroom to the kitchen or the living room carrying out her various chores, chatting all the while to the old man, who, sitting by the window, read the day's newspaper from cover to cover. Fifty minutes during which they talked about everything and nothing, serious and light-hearted matters, made small talk or discussed government policies, art or literature. Fifty minutes that were worth a thousand in the eyes of the young home help.

6

Ambroise arrived home from work to find Beth cooking a stew whose aroma filled the entire apartment. After cross-examining him as usual about his day, the elderly woman finally asked the question about her grandson's love life that had been tormenting her for a while. 'Have you seen your Julie again?' she asked innocently, stirring the meat with a spatula. No, Ambroise hadn't seen Julie again. Nor had he seen Manon, Lise or Laurine again. Girls had always been a problem. His grandmother despaired of his ever finding his soulmate. It wasn't for lack of opportunity. With his tall frame, angelic face and rebellious hair,

Ambroise never left the female sex indifferent. And without going as far as being a womanizer, the young man had been in love several times over the past few years, but each time the affair had ended after a matter of days – or weeks for the more serious relationships. Even though with time and experience Ambroise had learned to hedge around or keep quiet about his profession – to disguise it beneath a lie by saying, for instance, that he worked in the paramedical field – despite his precautions, the terrible moment always came when the word resurfaced: embalmer. Then, each time, a destructive process was set in motion which it was impossible to halt. First of all, the deluge of questions, the inevitable barrage of whys and hows. His replies generally aroused a feeling of revulsion at the idea that the same hands that caressed their body at night had spent the day poking cold, stiff corpses. Sometimes, on the contrary, the disclosure created a morbid attraction that wormed its way into the relationship like a maggot in an apple. But worst of all was the new way women looked at him, with a mixture of repugnance and fascination, when he came clean about his profession. Embalmer. The word tolled the end of the relationship. A waste, Beth would harp on, talking about the few girls who had passed the *kouign-amann* test. For the elderly lady, humanity was made up of two very different groups: people who liked the Breton cake and the rest. None of the conquests brought home by her grandson could escape Beth's *kouign-amann* test after the cheese course. For those who pursed their lips, avoided fats, the verdict was damning: a person incapable of appreciating the delectable buttery taste of a *kouign-amann* on the palate was incapable of receiving happiness in their heart! Those who did, which included Julie, were given her eternal blessing.

In the end, Ambroise had abandoned hope of finding a partner, preferring rather to wander in a sentimental wilderness interspersed from time to time with brief flings that had no future, pale substitutes for love with no other purpose than a shag. A physical experience, nothing more, and then escape before the word came and ruined it all once again. Sex without love, like a dish without salt. The other day, he had ventured to try the services of a professional. After finishing a job, as he walked back to the car park through the maze of little back streets in the driving rain, a young woman chewing gum paused to call out to him. 'Do you want to come upstairs?' A phrase from a B-movie. Long, shapely legs sheathed in nylon, sculptured breasts, bee-sting lips emphasized with gloss. Without thinking, Ambroise had followed her down the gloomy, stinking passageway and up a dozen stairs to the first floor where the tiny studio apartment served as a brothel. 'You pay in advance,' she commanded. He rummaged clumsily in his wallet for the fifty euros. 'Get undressed, big boy.' An order without warmth. Like a schoolteacher talking to a pupil. He had obeyed, feverishly folding his clothes and putting them on the chair. How many pairs of trousers, crumpled shirts, socks rolled into a ball and pairs of underpants had preceded his own clothes on that same seat?

'Lie down.'

The narrow bed was covered in protective paper, the sort you usually find on doctors', physiotherapists' and gynaecologists' examination tables.

'I'm an embalmer,' Ambroise had blurted out.

Why did he say that? He didn't know himself. Perhaps with the secret hope that the girl would throw him out like a scumbag, fling his fifty euros in his face and call him a pervert, telling him to go away and play with his dead bodies. But nothing of the sort happened.

'You do what you like, sweetheart,' the streetwalker replied as she rolled back his foreskin and gave him a mechanical hand job, expertly slipping a condom over his waning erection.

He shuddered. Clinical gestures. Ambroise tried to caress the young woman's breasts but she recoiled as if burned.

'No touching my breasts,' she said, deftly removing his hand. 'And no kissing,' she added. 'Unless you pay. Fifty's just for a blow job and a fuck.' All said in the tone of a shopkeeper admonishing an overly demanding customer.

When she took his penis in her mouth, he had the horrible feeling that it was merely a piece of meat, a cellophane-wrapped barbecue sausage detached from his own body. Then he clambered on top of her to penetrate her, and shuddered at the feel of the nylon stockings. The cold skin of a reptile. He closed his eyes to shut out the ceiling light flooding the bed, concentrating all his strength on desiring her and, after a laboured humping session, finally came inside this woman who'd been a stranger a few minutes earlier. An almost painful orgasm, triggered solely by the desire to get it over with as quickly as possible. The building had spat Ambroise out again into the street, an Ambroise disgusted at himself. Fifty euros, the price of damnation. He took a piping-hot shower and lathered his body for a long time. Beneath her perfume, she was the one who had reeked of death, not him.

7

As she often did, Madeleine Collot had already left her apartment building before Manelle's arrival and was limping up the street, her handbag slung over her shoulder. Her ninety-kilo bulk advanced with a rolling gait, her body trussed up in a raincoat that was much too small for her. Manelle hurried to join her and shield her with her umbrella, and relieve her of the wicker shopping basket dangling from her hand.

'Madeleine, how many times must I tell you to wait for me? You're really very naughty.'

The elderly lady was able to melt her home help's heart with her puppy eyes whenever Manelle scolded her. Once again, Manelle found it impossible to resist her client's contrite expression. Despite her advanced age, her obesity and her rheumatism, come wind, snow or rain like today, Madeleine Collot made it a point of honour to pay a daily visit to the local grocery store which was less than five hundred metres from her home. As stubborn as she was kind and reserved, nothing and nobody could dissuade her from this sacrosanct mission: going to Maxini's – 'Max choice, Mini prices'. Madeleine always took the same pleasure in entering the shop accompanied by her home help, whose job was to follow her like her shadow, the shopping basket within reach. It took fifteen minutes for her to buy a few things to keep her going until the next day's shopping expedition. 'I don't know how to explain it,' she once confessed to Manelle, who was asking her about this strange addiction. 'I find it helpful, you see. Before, I used to go to church, to morning mass, but there's no mass any more in the neighbourhood and no priest. So I make do with Maxini's. It's on the way to the church and it's always open. I don't know why but I find it comforting to see all those orderly, well-stocked shelves. I know it sounds silly, but it gives me a purpose for the next day. On Sundays, when it's closed, I don't feel right. I get anxious and the day seems much longer. I know a lot of widows who go and visit their husbands' graves at the cemetery on that day but me, my Dédé, I don't need to go and witter to a piece of polished granite for him to talk to me. I don't like cemeteries and I don't like Sundays,' she concluded.

Maxini's exuded abundance. The narrowness of the aisles added to this impression and every inch of shelf space was crammed to capacity. Intriguingly, Madeleine Collot's limp tended to disappear as she wandered up and down the laden aisles. Still today, the old lady's pace quickened as she plunged into the depths of the shop. Madeleine's purchases were confined to a veal escalope, a tub of celeriac remoulade, a litre of orange juice and four plain yoghurts. There was only one checkout at Maxini's, a till manned either by Bussuf, a young student who was always smiling and who loved joking, or by the manageress, a crabby, cold, ageless woman who always wore faded pink overalls. At Maxini's roulette, you could only bet on two options: Bussuf's smile or the manageress's pink. Today, it was the pink that won.

'Thirteen euros, twenty-eight cents,' snapped the boss, perched on her stool on casters.

The total rang out like a court sentence. After

rummaging frantically in her handbag, Madeleine had to face up to the fact: she'd left her purse at home. Manelle was moved by the panic in her eyes.

'Never mind, Madeleine, don't worry – you can pay me back later,' she reassured her as she held her credit card out to the cashier.

'I'm sorry, we don't take credit card payments for less than fifteen euros.'

The woman had spoken in a tone that brooked no argument. The till screen showed the total in luminous figures. One three point two eight. Manelle sighed.

'Madame Collot comes here every day, can't you make an exception?'

The lady tapped with her bony finger the little notice Sellotaped to the top of the till: *Credit cards accepted only for purchases over fifteen euros*. The adhesive had turned yellow with time and the felt tip had run in places. Manelle looked at the woman's name silk-screen-printed onto her overall before urging her again.

'Look, Ghislaine, I haven't got any cash on me, can you really not make an exception?'

No, Ghislaine clearly couldn't. Her head shook from right to left while her mouth emitted a string of tut-tut-tuts. Like an automatic sprinkler, thought Manelle.

'It doesn't matter,' stammered a shaken Madeleine to whom it mattered a great deal. She had never come back from Maxini's with an empty shopping basket.

'Yes, it does matter,' fumed Manelle.

The weekend hadn't soothed away her tiredness and she was in no mood to have her existence complicated by this skinny shrew. At the last team meeting, the section manager had once again drummed into them that individual initiatives weren't prohibited, provided the situation required it, of course. The situation required it. Madame Adding Machine wanted a minimum of fifteen euros, Manelle was going to give it to her. She spotted the sweet jar and the lollipop display by the till. There were treats of all colours and all shapes. Jelly beans, sherbet lemons, sugar-coated sweets, marshmallows, sweets to chew, sweets to suck, sweets that melt on the tongue. Sweets at two, three, four or five euro cents for the most expensive ones.

'How was your blood sugar last time you were tested, Madeleine?' asked Manelle.

'Good. It's my cholesterol that's a bit high, but my blood sugar's OK.'

'Right, you're going to give us one euro seventy-two's worth of sweets, please, Ghislaine. Thank you. A present from me,' she said to Madeleine, whose eyes began to light up.

The cashier had already plunged her claw into the first jar to extract a handful of liquorice wheels at five cents each. Manelle stopped her.

'Hold on, no, not those. Give us ten Haribo strawberries, four bananas . . . um . . . three bubble gums. We'll also have a handful of liquorice allsorts, five cola sweets, there . . . oh yes, some gummy crocodiles, they're yummy, crocodiles, give us eight crocodiles.'

The shopkeeper's hand flew from one jar to another, unscrewing the tops and screwing them back on following Manelle's instructions. Manelle paused for a moment.

'How much are we up to?' she simpered. 'We're not finished but we mustn't go over.'

After tapping nervously on her calculator, the manageress announced the score.

'That comes to ninety-five cents.'

Some of the other customers were starting to grow impatient and were muttering behind Manelle's back, to her great delight.

'Give us four chewy fruits, six Smurfs, two liquorice sweets, a cola Pasta Basta and two fried eggs. No, wait, just one fried egg and give us Dracula teeth instead. How much is that now?'

The keys clicked madly. The queue had grown even longer. There were rumblings of discontent.

'Has the till packed up?'

'What's going on?'

'What the hell's happening?'

Manelle turned around and offered the irritated customers a shrug to show her helplessness.

'One euro eighty-eight,' screeched Madame Adding Machine hysterically.

'It's too much,' replied Manelle, making her exchange one liquorice sweet and two crocodiles for a bubble gum, to ensure the total came to exactly fifteen euros.

The bony hand snatched the credit card and inserted it into the reader. On leaving, Manelle plonked the gummy Dracula teeth down in front of the cashier and flashed her most charming smile.

'For you. It will suit you perfectly.'

Madeleine walked down the street beside her home help clutching the precious bag of sweets. Reaching her safe haven, she limped over to her armchair and sank into it, sighing with contentment. From the kitchen where she was putting away the shopping, Manelle was rewarded by the childlike grin that lit up the old woman's face as she fished out a Haribo strawberry.

8

Again that evening, Beth had lectured him after dinner. 'If that's not a sorry sight, seeing a piece of furniture just sitting there gathering dust,' she'd scolded, jerking her chin in the direction of the bookcase. Ambroise recalled the entire afternoon he'd spent assembling the three flat-pack elements from Ikea. An afternoon unpacking and methodically sorting the various components and then meticulously following the assembly instructions. Almost three months had gone by since the brand-new white Hemnes bookcase had been installed against the sitting room wall. Not a week had gone by since without Beth complaining about the empty shelves which she found so sad. 'A bookcase without books is as ugly as a mouth without teeth,' she'd repeat. 'And makes no more sense than a graveyard without graves,' she'd add, with the utmost seriousness. 'You know where the books are, Ambroise. You have the key, all you need to do is go and get them,' she'd urge. Of course he knew where his books were. And of course he'd kept the set of keys his mother had given him when he'd moved out of his parents' home four years earlier. Only this was the thing: between the books and him was his father, Professor Henri Larnier.

Since his mother had passed away, Ambroise had never returned to the house in the upper part of the town. His mother, who had spent her entire life in the shadow of the great man, living vicariously in her gilded cage. Attentive to his every wish, anticipating his needs, she had ended up finding something resembling fulfilment in her boundless devotion to her illustrious husband. Wherever she was – at the baker's, the library, the theatre, the market, her hairdresser's – she was only ever known as Professor Henri Larnier's wife. And when he won the Nobel Prize in Medicine in 2005 for his work on the treatment of postoperative complications, Cécile Dumoulin, Larnier's spouse, had immediately been dubbed the-wife-of-Nobel-laureate-Henri-Larnier. That had become her name, for eternity. 'Whatever you do, don't tell Papa,' she'd murmured fearfully as she'd slipped the keys into her son's hand. For his mother, that gesture had been a real act of defiance, possibly the only one in her entire existence as an obedient wife. It was to remain their little secret, between a mother and her son. Ambroise had never needed to use the precious door key. Once a week, having ascertained that the great man was at work, Ambroise would park his car in a neighbouring street, walk anxiously up to the iron gates of number eight Rue Fenouillet, and steal in like a lover visiting his mistress. At the top of the steps, all he generally needed to do was push open the door left ajar for him and find his mother, hair freshly done and all dressed up. She would hug him tight for a long time then step back and give him that long, searching look common to all mothers when they are reunited with their child after too long an absence. The following hour would be spent chatting about this and that, reinventing the world over an orangeade or a glass of wine, and laughing while drinking each other in with their eyes. Neither ever mentioned his father during that hour. An hour that was theirs, and theirs alone. Being apart made them avid for each other's news. She wanted to know everything about his life, his work, his friends, his loves, about what Beth had lovingly cooked for him that week. He asked her about her health, her worries, the most recent film she'd seen or book she'd read. During those sixty minutes, the-wife-of-Nobel-laureate-Henri-Larnier was a woman like any other, with her desires, her joys and her sorrows. Each of these clandestine visits revitalized her. But she had kept from her son the disease that had surreptitiously come and lodged deep inside her one April day. Not wanting, perhaps, to mar that sacrosanct hour by telling him about the dull pain that had started to the left of her stomach and would not loosen its grip. She hadn't said anything to her husband either. Afraid of bothering the great man, perhaps; afraid, too, most likely of uttering the taboo word under that roof since Henri Larnier had banned all mention of medicine since his son's departure. She had also kept the signs of the cancer secret for as long as possible, putting her weight loss down to an imaginary diet, but by the time the symptoms had visibly erupted, it was too late. Metastasized into stage-four cancer, the beast had devoured her in less than two months. His father hadn't noticed anything.

The Nobel laureate in Medicine, the eminent surgeon who spent his days among tumours both malignant and benign, had not at any point troubled himself to detect the abomination that was eating up his own wife from within. On the day of the funeral, the father and son found themselves standing dazed on either side of the grave, contemplating without under-standing the chasm that separated them and which contained a lot more than the remains of a mother and wife. The idea of returning to that house repulsed Ambroise, but he had to. He had promised Beth. Tomorrow, he'd go and fetch his books.

9

Dividing his time between his oncology department at the hospital and being on call at the WHO in Geneva at the beginning of every week, his father was often away from home. Ambroise opened the gates and parked his car on the gravel driveway, in full view. He didn't want to sneak into the house like a thief. After all, he was Ambroise Larnier, the-son-of-Nobel-laureate-Henri-Larnier, and this was his home. As soon as he was inside, he flipped up the cover of the keypad on the wall and punched in the security code to deactivate the alarm, 12102005. The twelfth of October 2005, the date his father had been awarded the Nobel Prize. The code had remained unchanged all those years – the sin of pride. Ambroise walked through the sitting room and half opened the bay window that looked out onto the terrace. The pleasant fragrance of freshly mown grass wafted up from the lawn. Beyond it, the turquoise water in the swimming pool glinted in the sunlight. Water where no one swam any more, he was certain. As far back as he could remember, he could not recall a day when he hadn't seen his father in his swimming trunks. 'A swimming pool without bathers is like a car park without cars, it's sad and useless!' Beth would have said. The house looked as if it had just undergone a massive spring clean. Cold and immaculate were the two adjectives that came into Ambroise's mind as he contemplated the living room. It lacked the warmth his mother had brought to the home when she was alive. A vase of flowers on a sideboard, cushions scattered on a couch with deliberate casualness, a half-open book on an armrest, magazines on the coffee table, an incense stick slowly burning, a fruit basket, a half-completed cross-word – so many signs of a human presence that were no longer there. On all the walls there were photos of his father. His father posing with a minister, his father shaking hands with a president, his father being honoured by his peers, his father and his Nobel Prize, his father in a white coat at the opening of a new oncology department. And everywhere, carefully framed or placed on shelves, certificates, awards and press cuttings singing his praises. No trace of his mother or of Ambroise in this temple to the glory of the man of science. He paused for a moment by the kitchen and smiled ruefully at the sight of the round table that had witnessed so much shouting, so many words hurled in each other's faces, where so many unspoken things between a father and a son had been held back as they tore each other apart at mealtimes in front of a helpless mother and wife.

Saddling your child with the same name as the famous father of modern surgery, Ambroise Paré, spoke volumes about the father's aspirations for his son. But the boy, then the adolescent and later the young man, had never lived up to his illustrious genitor's ambitions. At fifteen, to his father's great displeasure, Ambroise gave up learning the piano for the guitar, the electric guitar to boot, ditching Wolfgang Amadeus Mozart for Angus Young without any qualms. At eighteen, he passed his baccalaureate but didn't gain the distinction or merit expected by Henri Larnier. After repeating his first year of medicine, the young man dashed his father's hopes once and for all by enrolling at the regional nursing school. The final blow came a little later when, after two hospital placements, Ambroise informed his parents one December evening that he couldn't bear the suffering of the living but considered on the other hand that taking care of the bodies of the deceased was among the noblest of professions. 'Embalmer!' his father had spluttered, beside himself. How could Ambroise Larnier, his own son, stoop to practise the second oldest profession in the world after that of prostitute? 'If you're interested in the dead, go and join them but don't you dare set foot in this house ever again!' the Nobel laureate had yelled, verging on apoplexy. Ambroise had packed his bags, embraced his sobbing mother and left the house without a glance at the man with whom he had never shared anything other than shouting or disappointment. Beth had taken him in without bombarding him with questions, had let him move into the back bedroom and made him a *kouign-amann* to cheer him up.

Ambroise climbed the stairs and went into his old bedroom. Nothing had changed since his departure. Same posters on the walls, the furniture all in the same place. Post-it notes that had been there for four years were plastered over the blotter on the desk. A museum, he thought. My museum. His mother had kept the room as it had been, with the secret hope that one day he would come back and live in the family home again. The shelves on the wall were sagging under the weight of the books. All his comic album series were there. *Trolls of Troy*, *Asterix*, the complete set of *Tintin*. Below them, the writers who had been his nocturnal companions during his adolescence. Stephen King, J. K. Rowling, Tolkien. Airport novels, in his father's view. Ambroise opened the two large bags he had brought with him and gently placed the books inside. After two journeys to the boot of his car, he checked that he hadn't left any tell-tale clues and locked the front door. A prison, he thought as he reset the alarm. My father lives in a prison.

10

Obsessed with hygiene, Ghislaine de Montfaucon had elevated the art of cleanliness to a religion and was intransigent when it came to such matters. It wasn't enough to wipe your feet when you entered the affluent home located in the heart of the old town. A basket full of disposable blue plastic overshoes awaited the visitor next to the doormat. Manelle grabbed a pair and slipped them on before going any further.

'I'm in here, Mademoiselle Flandin. Leave the washing-up, we can see to that later.'

As usual, thought Manelle, gliding to the dining room on the polished parquet floor. The elderly lady was waiting for her, already seated at the table in front of the Scrabble board, impatient to continue the game they had begun three days earlier. In truth, Ghislaine de Montfaucon asked nothing more of her home helps than to be her Scrabble partner for an hour. Some of Manelle's colleagues had complained about it. But not her – she far preferred an hour of Scrabble, draughts or Ludo to an hour of ironing or housework. Once again Ghislaine de Montfaucon was about to win the game hands down because, as well as being neurotic, she was the queen of cheats. A mistress in the art of making up words, she invented their definitions which eventually became real to her, and only to her. Each time her powers of self-persuasion left Manelle gobsmacked. A GRIJAK? Of course, you know, a grijak is a primitive bear with very thick fur that roamed the northern regions of America during the Ice Age. TORQAD? Torqad is a dish based on corn and goat that is eaten on the Tibetan Plateau. Very flavoursome, apparently. Some words spawned other words. To HEXUFF: an action consisting of polishing steel with a hexuffer, a spatula-shaped tool. Manelle had long been closing her eyes to these neologisms that were pure invention. Just as she no longer mentioned the disappearance of certain letters from her stand, often vowels replaced by consonants, or the addition of fictitious double-word-score squares in favour of the old lady when it was time to count their points. Today again, Ghislaine de Montfaucon was unable to stop herself from indulging in her tricks, not even waiting until Manelle had sat down to place a new word on the board.

'MALITH. Double-word score, which gives me twenty-two points,' she crowed. 'Your turn, mademoiselle.'

Manelle refrained from pointing out that it had been her turn to go first, if her memory was correct, and she also decided not to mention that MALITH with a double-word score came to twenty, not twenty-two points. As for the meaning of the word itself, she did not even have the pleasure of asking its inventor, because Ghislaine de Montfaucon, a widow and fit as a fiddle for her ninety-two years, hastened to enlighten her. The malith is a very hard stone found on the slopes of volcanoes. Manelle smiled as she turned over her tiles. The letters A and U which would have enabled her to make SPATULA had miraculously been transformed into a G and an H. Using the A from MALITH, she made do with TAGS and drew three tiles from the cotton pouch. Tiles which, once a month, were washed thoroughly and dried one by one to keep them sparkling clean. Hygiene was no laughing matter for Ghislaine de Montfaucon.

11

The hospital morgue was in the basement, on level -2. Ambroise stepped inside the spacious lift and pressed the button. Beneath the smell of disinfectant coming off the walls lurked the acrid stench of corpses, which grew increasingly persistent as the lift descended. It was an oily smell that clung to your skin, your clothes and your hair and which, he knew from having experienced it many times, would pervade his sinuses and lodge behind his forehead to haunt him even after he was back in the open air. A smell of abomination. The best definition he'd ever heard of those emanations had been whispered to him by an elderly stretcher bearer: smells you shouldn't look at.

'Well, well, it's Monsieur Ambroise in person!'

Ambroise was always delighted to see Boubacar and Abelardo, the two morgue attendants. One was black and brawny and the other pale and puny. 'My brother from another mother,' Boubacar would often joke while his colleague looked on wearily. When asked what they did for a living, they would reply 'morgue attendant and apnoea specialist', which profoundly baffled the questioner. The two buddies knew a thing or two about holding their breath because when they opened some of the containers they had to do so for a long time. This basement was their realm, their second home. You didn't go to the hospital morgue, you went down to Bouba and Abel's.

Perpetually clad in their green overalls – not the surgeon's green, no, a horticultural green, the Senegalese attendant would always point out with the utmost seriousness – they never left their burrow except to go up to the wards to collect the dead, store the bodies in the containers and take them out on request, receive the undertakers, prepare the prayer room and greet the families. For all of them – pathologists, undertakers, embalmers, the deceased's relatives – Boubacar and

Abelardo were the gatekeepers. They were the custodians of the temple and the morgue's living memory. The two friends knew each one of the occupants of the eighteen drawers in the long-stay room, the one reserved for the forensic institute. Madame Mangin in number nine left yesterday for burial. Monsieur Dompart in number twelve is to be re-examined by the pathologist tomorrow.

The small room where they spent the greater part of their time was a bright, colourful island. The walls were covered in postcards of turquoise seas, mountain vistas, photos of laughing women and children, weddings and celebrations. Images of life above, far from the world below and its smells you shouldn't look at. Bunches of flowers everywhere made the place look cheery. Armfuls of carnations, roses and tulips of all colours, and floral arrangements not claimed by the families generally ended up here. This room was their raft, a raft bursting with life in the middle of a lake of stagnant, oily water. Bouba got up from the table and gave Ambroise a bear hug, crushing him to his breast.

'How's my young white witch doctor? Still rousing the dead?'

'It's what I do best,' retorted Ambroise, extricating himself from Bouba's bear hug to embrace Abel.

'Will you have a bite with us? You've got the time, it's just a cosmetic job and the family won't be here before three p.m.'

'That's kind of you but I've already had lunch.'

The two morgue attendants ate all day long. Whatever the hour, the table in the centre of their cubbyhole was always laden with food. Today, home-made puff-pastry parcels sat next to fried cassava. Ambroise wondered how it was possible to savour any food in a place like this. 'Believe it or not, you can cope with the smells better on a full stomach,' Bouba had once said to him. Ambroise accepted the glass of wine that Abel was holding out to him, a rioja produced by a Spanish cousin near Penedès. 'Heard the one about the pathologist being interviewed by a journalist?' asked Bouba. 'The hack asks: "Doctor, how many autopsies have you carried out on dead bodies?" and the pathologist answers: "All my autopsies have been carried out on dead bodies".' Ambroise smiled. He enjoyed Bouba's often cynical wisecracks. It was a strange phenomenon, this contrast between the exuberance of the two morgue attendants and the environment in which they worked, as if the fact of being in constant contact with the dead heightened their love of life.

'I put your customer in room three. Here's the bag

of clothes,' added Bouba, holding out the suit in its protective cover. Don't look for the shoes, there aren't any. His dentures are on the trolley.'

Ambroise walked up the corridor to the treatment room. Already undressed, the deceased, an Asian man of seventy-two, was covered with just a sheet. There were bruises from the drip on his wrist and Ambroise could decipher on his neck the vestiges of a tracheotomy. His body was disturbingly thin. Cancer had the distinctiveness of emptying its host, drying up faces, devouring the fat and then the flesh, leaving to the Grim Reaper nothing but a skeletal body stuffed with medicines. Devoured from the inside by the gruesome beast, thought Ambroise. On the slightly distended abdomen, a pretty green patch was spreading, a sign that bacteria were already present and ready to invade the body. Even if the remains deserved the full treatment, in Ambroise's view, the family had decided to restrict the intervention to the bare necessities; the funeral was scheduled for the following day. He checked the identity of the deceased then put on his protective clothing to begin the grooming. Ambroise had no difficulty in flexing the body, as rigor mortis had not found many muscles in which to sink its claws. The Master liked to cite the following Czech proverb when he found himself in the presence of a corpse that was all skin and bones: 'When there's nothing, there's nothing even for death to take.' He cleaned the eyes and nose before draining the orifices. He put the dentures back in, sutured the neck where the tracheotomy had punctured it and placed patches over the eyes. Having sewn up the mouth, Ambroise washed the deceased from head to toe with a disinfectant solution. With his fingertips he rubbed moisturizing cream inside the lips. The man weighed less than forty kilos, so dressing him took no more than a few minutes. His dark skin required no particular make-up. A light comb-through was enough to plaster his wispy hair to the top of his head. He slipped the cushion under the dead man's neck to raise his head. Dressed in a fine anthracite-grey suit, with a tie, the skeletal corpse that had confronted him on his arrival had regained a semblance of humanity in less than half an hour. He pulled the sheet up to the chest. Not knowing the deceased's religion, Ambroise merely placed his hands on top of the fabric, without joining them. Satisfied, he put away his things and dropped in to say goodbye to the masters of the house and tell them that they could take the body up to the presentation room. He found

Bouba alone, eating a slice of tart and reading the latest *Canard enchaîné*.

'I'm done. Say goodbye to Abel for me.'

'Come back whenever you like, you're at home here, young white witch doctor! And don't ever forget this: only dead fish swim with the current!'

Boubacar's hearty laugh echoed as in a cathedral, following Ambroise into the lift.

12

On 18 September, Ambroise had an appointment to visit Isabelle de Morbieux, as he'd done every year for the past four years. The retirement home, Le Clos de la Roselière, stood among the wooded hills to the north of the town. After driving several kilometres along a winding road, he turned his van onto the tree-lined avenue that led to the residence. The opulent building came into view bathed in the afternoon sunshine and surrounded by carefully manicured lawns. White marble benches were dotted around in the shade of majestic oaks. The expression 'retirement home' was never uttered in this place. It must have been among the words that were banned because they might remind the residents that they were elderly people who had reached the end of their lives. In this type of place, a pressure-relief mattress was called a 'comfort accessory'. Disguise the fact that this was a place to die beneath the veneer of elegance and the gilding of a luxury residence – that was the stated aim of La Roselière. Everything here gave the illusion of a peaceful future in a delightful environment, surrounded by staff who were both biddable and competent, the only sounds being the twittering of the many birds nesting in the copses in the grounds. A magnificent optical illusion, thought Ambroise as he entered the lobby. He believed he could read the same weary resignation on most of the faces of the residents he passed. Despite the size of their wallets, and the effort and resources deployed to delay the moment, there was no doubt that decay eventually set in here as elsewhere. In the coolness of clean sheets and beneath the high ceilings, amid the bustle of the cleaners and the nurses, the gentle hum of the air conditioning in summer and the warmth exuded by the radiators in winter, people ended up caving inwards, their senses dissolving in the softness of the carpets.

He ignored the lift and bounded up the wide

staircase with a light step. The rooms on the second floor all had the names of flowers. Iris, Gladiola, Pansy, Daffodil, Edelweiss, Hibiscus. Ambroise always wondered, not without a smile, if there were any rooms called Thistle, Dandelion or Nettle. Orchid was right at the end of the vast corridor. He rapped twice. A clear voice invited him in. Apart from a handful of centenarians, the colony consisted mostly of nonagenarians, among them Isabelle de Morbieux. Ambroise recalled the first time he had set foot in this place, four years earlier. 'No need for any equipment,' Roland Bourdin had said, 'living client. An *Elysium Plus*,' he'd added, with a note of respect. 'She asked to see you, don't let her down. Contracts like this, you know, don't grow on trees.' The *Elysium Plus*, the only formula for which Roland Bourdin deigned to use the definite article and a plethora of adjectives. This Rolls-Royce of contracts was ideal for clients like Isabelle de Morbieux who wanted to arrange everything while they were alive so as not to leave the task of organizing the final journey to others. A top-end, turnkey post-mortem formula, with funeral services reflecting the exorbitant price. Noble wood coffin, fine silk padding, music and plentiful Gregorian chants playing while the body is displayed in the chapel of rest, designing the announcement and printing three hundred cards on 200 gsm satin paper, provision of a giant wreath of fresh flowers, fine gold engraving on the plaque, supply of two finely engraved ciboria with candles, the release of doves on leaving the cemetery, a condolence book with vellum pages and lambskin cover and – the icing on the cake – complete preservation of the body carried out by an experienced professional. That was why Isabelle de Morbieux had asked to meet the embalmer who would perform the procedure. Ambroise had encountered a sharp mind in a tired body. At over ninety, the elderly lady had lost her aristocratic bearing and could only walk with a Zimmer frame, and she even used a wheelchair to go into the grounds, but her face still had an extraordinary youthfulness and the film that time annoyingly places over the eyes of the elderly had not yet marred the brightness of her gaze. But the most surprising thing was her voice, a strangely clear voice which it was hard to believe could come from such a frail body. She had not concealed her surprise at finding out how young Ambroise was, confessing that she had been expecting to meet one of those old professors in corduroy trousers rather than a youth who looked like a barely pubescent medical student and not the experienced professional mentioned in the contract. He had re-assured her as to his skills, telling her that if Bourdin & Sons had entrusted him and no one else with this assignment, it was chiefly because of his recognized expertise. He neglected to mention that it was also, and above all, because he was the only person available when the funeral directors had called. Even so, Isabelle de Morbieux had been dubious as to his ability to take care of her body properly when the time came. She had bombarded him with questions clearly intended to put his professional know-how to the test. Some-what infuriated, Ambroise had ended up spouting the famous expression that the Master was in the habit of declaiming from his podium to his students: 'No client has ever complained about me during their life-time.' Contrary to all expectations, the old woman had burst out laughing. From that moment, the ice had been broken and the conversation had continued in the most amicable way. Isabelle de Morbieux expected him to proceed like an artist with his model. 'I want you to get to know my wrinkles while I'm alive,' she'd told him. 'I want you to immerse yourself in me now, all the better to reconstitute me when the day comes.' She had shown him the cosmetics she used, the way she did her hair. Then she'd told him about her young days, her life as a woman before the autumn had come and withered her flesh and her senses. Her husband departed too soon, her daughter who came every Sunday and took her for lunch in town, her grandchildren and great-grandchildren, whose colourful drawings covered an entire wall of her room. An hour and a half later – the time for a treatment, Ambroise had thought – she bade him goodbye, not without making him promise to come back the following year, same day, same time, for which he would be paid. The old lady was making an appointment with her embalmer as she would with her cardiologist, her ophthalmologist, her pedicurist or her dentist. 'For a check-up,' she'd added mischievously.

So every year on Isabelle de Morbieux's birthday, Ambroise walked into Orchid room on the dot of three. She would be waiting for him curled up in her armchair, with a bulky Bible sitting on her scrawny thighs. 'I have never come across a better novel than this one,' she explained, closing the book. 'Action, suspense, intrigue, the fantastic, baddies, goodies, it's all there,' she said admiringly. Ambroise smiled. This woman was like those very old plum trees which, despite their cracked trunks and dry, crumbly bark, are reborn every spring to produce the best fruits come summer. She inquired after his health. He asked her in return how the past twelve months had been for her. 'Like a long winter by the fireside,' she replied. Neither mentioned the main reason for his visit. The old woman merely showed Ambroise a new wrinkle that had appeared, the latest liver spot on the right side of her forehead, discussed with him the way to use a little more foundation there to conceal the indelible mark. Often, Ambroise simply listened, letting her talk about herself. 'I'm bored,' she confessed. 'Boredom can be painful, you know. It sets in surreptitiously then haunts your days and your nights like a dull ache that you can never shake off. It stabs you sometimes, making you cry, then ebbs, it goes, it comes, but in the end, you have to live with it because boredom, when you're ninety-four, isn't the same as when you're twenty. There's room for it to take root and weave in and out of your memories and your regrets, to fill the voids. It is a drowning that only ends with your last breath. But knowing that I will be in good and beautiful hands when the time comes, I am much less afraid of death, you know. Come, that's enough about me. Let's drink instead to your youth and your future, young man,' concluded the old woman, jerking her chin in the direction of the mini fridge that gave out a constant hum in a corner of the room. Each year they shared the same ritual with a bottle of Clairette de Die and a plate of macaroons. They clinked glasses, flute against flute, and crunched the biscuits in silence. Life outside entered the room through the half-open window in a joyful chirruping. When it was time for him to leave, Isabelle De Morbieux held Ambroise's hand between her bony fingers a little longer than usual.

'I am happy to know that it will be you, Ambroise.'

'Me what?' he answered, perplexed.

'The last man to see me naked and to take care of my body.'

There was nothing salacious in these words. They were just the expression of her sincere relief. For the first time, he detected a change in the old woman's voice. It was the somewhat subdued voice of a person making ready to depart.

13

'Wakey, wakey, lovebirds,' shouted Manelle cheerfully as she always did when she went into the Fourniers' bedroom and drew back the heavy curtains to let in a ray of light. Because when it came to being in love, Hélène and Aimé Fournier were as besotted as during the early days of their marriage. And although they had slept in separate beds for more than a year, they still insisted on being in the same room, side by side. A hospital bed with a hoist for her, a single bed for him. Manelle waited until the elderly woman had finished raising herself up with the help of the trapeze bar and then pivoted her slowly into a sitting position.

'Shall I bring your walking frame?' asked Manelle, even though she already knew the answer.

'He's my walking frame,' replied Hélène Fournier, gazing fondly at the love of her life who edged around the bed to offer her the support of his arm, as he did every morning.

Manelle bustled around making breakfast and soon the smell of toast filled the kitchen. She loved to start the day helping this delightful couple. Hélène Fournier was a resolute optimist. 'Fifty-eight years ago, we vowed for better or for worse, and even when it seems that all that's left is the worst, you can still find a little of the best,' she'd say. 'You just have to make the effort.' The couple stayed afloat by clinging to each other. She was the head, he the feet, a wobbly tandem that got through the days, come what may. Hélène spoke for both of them, read, watched TV, concocted tasty little dishes, managed their affairs, kept the household accounts – all things which her reduced mobility in no way prevented her from doing. Meanwhile, Aimé dozed most of the time, despite his wife's great efforts to keep him awake by asking him to do countless little jobs for her during the day. Go and fetch some potatoes from the pantry. Put the cheque book back in the desk drawer. Bring her book from the bedside table. Bring her a comb from the bathroom.

Help her to go to the toilet. Come and give her a kiss. 'It's for his own good,' she told Manelle. 'His body's still fine, you know, it's his head that's gone. He'd sleep all day long if I let him, and one day he just wouldn't wake up again,' she added on a serious note. Manelle put the two pill dispensers in front of Hélène, who flipped up the lids of the Thursday compartments with her thumb. 'The daily pill dispenser is the old person's diary,' she said as she aligned the four morning tablets on the tablecloth in front of her Aimé, enumerating them: 'The blue one for your blood pressure, the purple one for your cholesterol, the green one for your circulation and the yellow one for your urea. You just need an orange, an indigo and a red one and you'll have all the colours of the rainbow, my poor darling,' she remarked sadly. She meanwhile was entitled to three pills which she washed down with a big gulp of *café au lait*. She spread a piece of toast with redcurrant jelly and slid it in front of her husband. Manelle took advantage of the ten minutes that breakfast lasted to make the beds and air the bedroom. Ten minutes during which the kitchen was filled with the sounds of slurping and chewing made by the Fourniers avidly bolting down their slices of toast.

Before going into the bathroom, Hélène carefully selected the clothes they would wear that day. For her and for Aimé. A ritual Manelle threw herself into with the joy of a little girl dressing up her dolls. If the old woman took pride in her appearance, it was also, and above all, part of her determination not to let herself go. Letting oneself go was the enemy. 'A stealthy foe that soon takes over if you're not careful,' she told Manelle one morning. 'You start by getting your hair done less often, you stop wearing make-up, you forget to cut your nails, you stop plucking your eyebrows and you end up looking like nothing on earth.' She, Hélène Fournier, had seen friends who had let go one fine day and slid into neglect without realizing it, before disappearing altogether. While Aimé took himself into the living room to slump in his armchair and have his first snooze of the day, Manelle flung open the wardrobe doors in front of Hélène, who concentrated hard. Shelves and rail on the right, her clothes; shelves and rail on the left, her husband's. Side by side, like the beds.

'I'll wear the blue blouse, the floral one, it's going to be warm today. With the beige trousers.'

'Do you want the light blue silk scarf as well?' suggested Manelle.

'No, it'll be too tone-on-tone with the blouse. Take the orange one instead. And for Aimé, give him a pair of jeans. I know he doesn't like them, but they make him look younger. They'll be perfect with the white shirt. And give him the grey waistcoat, he's always cold.'

When everything was laid out, Hélène sent Manelle to fetch Aimé to wash and dress him. The vast walk-in shower installed at great expense when the old lady saw that the condition of her legs was deteriorating awaited them. The Fourniers took their shower together, Hélène sitting on the folding seat and Aimé standing beside her. They soaped each other, caressing with the washcloths each other's bodies which they knew inside out, splashing, shampooing, laughing sometimes. When Aimé had finished, Manelle came back into the bathroom to dress Hélène. Despite her experience, she always struggled with putting on the flesh-coloured elastic support socks. She said to herself that the guy who invented them must never have had to put them on a granny aged over eighty with ankles as stiff as a board and calves as fat as thighs. Ten minutes later, primped and made up as if for her first dance, Hélène Fournier came out on Manelle's arm, ready to attack a new day. From the sitting room came the sound of Aimé's heavy snoring, from the vast depths of his weary spirit, before his loving wife brought him back to life asking him to bring her a litre of milk from the pantry, or the TV magazine open at the crossword page.

14

Ambroise recoiled slightly on coming across the fluffy ginger ball nestling between the calves of the deceased and glowering at him. When anyone tried to move the one-eyed cat from its place, it dug its claws into the dead man's pyjamas. Ambroise had to chase the creature with a broom and clap his hands to get it to leave the room. The tomcat fled to the kitchen, spitting and hissing, and then vanished into the garden through the half-open French window. None of the family members present wanted to take in the mangy tom who was over sixteen years old. As often happened, the death of the master had sealed the fate of the cat. An appointment had already been made with the local vet to give him an injection the day after the funeral. Ambroise slipped on his overalls and got down to the task in hand. It took him less than an hour and a quarter to treat the body. After giving the sparse hair a final once-over with a comb, he put away his equipment, removed his gloves, mask and overalls, loaded the car and took his leave. That evening, the theatre company was performing. Just time to have a quick shower and bolt down the food that Beth was bound to have waiting for him, then he'd head off to the village where the show was taking place. Must remember to refill the vanity case with bottles of make-up remover. He was just thinking about that when the thing sprang out from between his feet as he stopped at a red light. The tomcat gave a hoarse mew, soon drowned out by Ambroise's yells when the animal started climbing up his right leg, digging its claws in through his trousers. He grabbed the cat by the scruff of the neck and pulled it off his calf, then threw it onto the floor mat on the passenger side. Huddled up, its ears lying back, the creature stared at him with its one eye. Its ginger fur was striped with battle scars. A long gash ran from its left ear to its nose in a mocking grin. Its tail, which was missing a third, made its scraggy body look unbalanced. Its dull, matted fur did not make you want to stroke it. A veteran fighter who must have taken part in all the neighbourhood battles, reckoned Ambroise. He didn't know what to do. Take it back to where it had come from? The tom hadn't survived so many fights to end up in the hands of a man in a white coat who was going to inject him with a one-way ticket to join his master. Abandon it by throwing it out of the car and letting fate take care of it? He would never forgive himself. Honking from the car behind him jolted Ambroise back into the moment. He parked his van by the roadside and, without really thinking, grabbed one of the cases and started emptying it of its contents. He put on several pairs of gloves, armed himself with courage, grabbed the cat and stuffed it into the case, then hastily fastened the leather flaps. Oblivious to the persistent caterwauling coming from the case, Ambroise set off again and stopped at the first supermarket he came to. He stood staring at the cat food section for ages without being able to make up his mind. The five metres of shelving, two metres high, offered an infinite variety of tinned and dry food. Chicken, beef, vegetable, fish flavoured, in chunks, or pâté. He finally decided on biscuits. The pictures of cats on the packaging all outdid each other in beauty.

Precious faces of competition animals, stars with fur that you wanted to plunge your hand into, fur that was a far cry from the specimen that he had just taken into his care. Each packet had its type of cat. Sterilized, kittens, tubby, indoor. No one-eyed moth-eaten toms. He picked up the bag of biscuits recommended for elderly cats. Ambroise chucked into the trolley the first cat tray within reach, added two bags of super-absorbent, wood-scented litter and headed for the checkout.

Twenty minutes later, he opened the door of the apartment and immediately released the cat from its makeshift jail. As he feared, the welcome Beth gave the tom took the form of a firm and definitive pro-nouncement that must have resonated throughout the building.

'No animals under my roof!'

'But I thought it was dogs you didn't like,' retorted Ambroise.

'The two aren't mutually exclusive, Ambroise Larnier.'

When Beth called him by his full name, it did not bode well.

'Besides, have you seen the evil look in its eye? And its sly grin?'

'You can see that's a scar.'

'Scar maybe, but in any case, he really is an ugly old thing.'

'Haven't you always told me not to judge people by their looks, Nana?'

'Admit that your wounded soldier doesn't exactly make you want to stroke him. And stop calling me Nana, you know I hate that.'

'Just for a few days, please, just a few days, till I find a solution.'

'I don't see what solution you'll be able to find with its face. Look at its fur! Never seen a mog like it.'

Completely oblivious to this argument even though it was of the utmost relevance to him, the mog in question was polishing off the plate of cat food that Ambroise had put down for him on arrival. He set up the litter tray in the passage under Beth's disapproving eye, took the time to wash his instruments and dived into the shower. Beth ambushed him as he came out.

'What's more, I wouldn't be surprised if the mangy fur of that animal of yours isn't ridden with fleas!'

'One, it's not *my* animal. It's hardly my fault if the cat preferred my car and freedom to the lethal jab at the vet's. Two, first thing tomorrow I'll run out and buy the best anti-flea treatment, I promise.'

'And he'd better not try to mark his territory by spraying his pee all over the place. I wouldn't survive that and nor would he!'

'Listen, Beth, we'll talk about it tomorrow. I've got to run, they're relying on me and I don't want to be late. I won't be back before one o'clock in the morning. A *far breton* or a *kouign-amann*?' asked Ambroise, grabbing the still-warm plate covered in aluminium foil.

'An apple tart, that's all you deserve.'

He kissed Beth, who was grumpier than ever, and left the old woman and the tom glaring at each other in silent confrontation.

15

That morning, there was no 'my little turtle dove' or 'my Tinker Bell' to greet Manelle's arrival. She found Samuel slumped listlessly on a chair in the kitchen, his gaze absent. In front of him was a large blue envelope and on top of it the result of his tests. Grams and milligrams per litre, percentages, units, graphs, coloured curves. On the table were spread various images of his brain. On several of the scans, you could see a lighter patch like the eye of a cyclone in the midst of the grey. Without being a specialist, you could immediately see that the ugly patch had no business being there, that it was a blot on the landscape. Manelle gently moved the envelope aside and grasped the old man's hands. For nearly ten minutes, she comforted him, explaining that all this didn't tell them much, that he should wait to see the specialist to find out what it really meant. Samuel told her about the pain that was now permanently locked up inside his skull. How, even at night, he knew it was there, crouching behind his forehead, hiding, waiting for the daylight to strike his retinas before unfurling anew. He told her how the horrible MRI tunnel had completely swallowed up his body and then, on leaving the examination, the words of the man in white, all those words he hadn't understood and had got muddled up in his head. Manelle pictured the old man coming out of the ordeal distressed and confused, clutching his blue envelope, getting into the patient transport ambulance to be taken home. 'When do you have to go back and see the neurologist?' she asked.

'Monday afternoon, at three o'clock. I've got to order hospital transport,' added the old man in a flat voice.

'I'll take you,' said Manelle in a tone that brooked no argument. And as she tidied away the documents, she glimpsed the words in bold across the bottom of the page, like a death sentence: *glioblastoma multiforme*.

16

The key to the funeral parlour was under the flower pot on the window ledge, on the courtyard side, as the receptionist had told him over the telephone. The woman had informed him that the deceased's daughters would be bringing his clothes over at around two o'clock. 'Pacemaker to be removed,' she added, before hanging up. Another one who used words sparingly, thought Ambroise with a smile. He let himself in and went over to the cold store. The deceased was in the second compartment. He slid out the drawer, opened the body bag and checked the man's identity against the label on the door of the compartment. Serge

Condrieux, aged seventy-nine. Died in his sleep during the night. Death often had the annoying habit of draining people's faces then filling them out and refashioning them as it pleased. In Serge Condrieux's case, it hadn't had the time. His face was peaceful, with no sign of suffering. The illusion of a lovely death, as if it were possible for a death of any kind to be lovely. Ambroise transferred the body to the trolley and wheeled him into the treatment room. As he broke the rigor mortis, he read the history of the body in the scars life had left on the flesh. Above the groin, an old appendicectomy scar. At the base of the neck, the barely visible traces of thyroid surgery. The characteristic imprint of a BCG vaccination at the top of the left arm. The little finger on his right hand was missing, leaving only a pinkish stump, a vestige of an accident. To the touch, Ambroise could feel the callouses on the palms even through his gloves. A manual worker's hands, he guessed. A tanned complexion and deep wrinkles spoke of a life spent outdoors. The bulge under the skin beneath the left collarbone indicated the position of the pacemaker. Ambroise made an incision in the skin in order to remove the device. He put it with the three others stored in the plastic box which he emptied once a week into a special collection bin. No pacemakers in the afterlife, that was the rule. Whether it was heaven or hell, cremation or burial, lithium batteries had no place there.

The sound of footsteps echoed through the funeral home. Ambroise put down his instruments for a moment to go and greet the two middle-aged women walking down the corridor. Although tired, their faces didn't yet bear signs of grief. In the hours following the death, action sometimes prevented the family from thinking about the emptiness of loss. Informing the relatives, dealing with the funeral arrangements, and organizing the day and the time of the funeral with the priest were all things that needed to be done and which delayed the onset of tears for a while. As they handed him the clothes, he reassured them, saying that he would take the greatest care of their father's body. The one who seemed to be the younger of the two spoke.

'We would very much like him to wear this,' she said, taking a red plastic ball from her pocket.

Perplexed, Ambroise stared at the object the size of an apricot that the woman had just slipped into his hand. It was only when her sister showed him the photo that he understood. The man was portrayed in full clown costume. A tiny pink hat, eyes and mouth outlined in white, giant bow tie, multi-coloured suit and outsize yellow shoes, not forgetting the vital red nose. Then they began to talk, telling him how when they were little, every Christmas, their father would bring the presents disguised not as Santa Claus, but as a clown, a crazy clown who made them laugh till they cried. He had kept up that joyous tradition ever since, Christmas after Christmas, with his grandchildren and great-grandchildren, improving his performance each year, egged on by the kids' excited shrieks, and the entire family called him Grandpa Clown. Ambroise listened to them pouring out their hearts, reminiscing between tears and laughter.

'We'd really like to see him with his red nose, you see,' the older sister concluded.

'What about his clothes?' ventured Ambroise. 'Wouldn't you like to see him dressed in his clown suit and made up like in your photo?'

'We didn't think it was possible,' the deceased's daughters chorused enthusiastically. 'We've got his costume in the car. We wanted to put it in the coffin with him but if you could dress him in it and make him up, that would be wonderful,' added the younger one.

The eldest sister was already coming back with the

clown suit and accessories. Ambroise took them from her, reassured the two women one last time and invited them to come back after an hour or so, the time it would take him to finish off and dress their father. As soon as he had completed the germicidal treatment, Ambroise made the last sutures and washed the body before dressing it. He placed the bib over the vest, slid the deceased's legs into the too-short and abnormally wide trousers, rolled on the striped socks that came to the top of his calves, laced up the shoes that gaped at the toes, raised the dead man's torso while he clipped on the braces and eased him into the multi-coloured spotted jacket. Getting his hands into the white gloves was a struggle. Then Ambroise took out the cosmetics bag and, aided by the photo, made up the dead man's face. He used the round brush to apply the rouge, the sponge to outline the mouth and eyes in white, pencilled in false black eyebrows, and redefined the lips, stretching them into a merry grin. He clamped the orange wig onto the head, tied the enormous bow tie around his neck, slipped the big plastic daisy into the jacket buttonhole and plonked the little pink hat on the chest, next to the folded hands. Then, Ambroise gently held the red plastic ball between his thumb and forefinger and put it on the nose of Serge Condrieux, alias Grandpa Clown. The result was striking. He folded up the body bag, arranged the velvet drape around the corpse, slid the cushion under the deceased's head and wheeled the trolley into the funeral parlour. He put the frame and the photo on the pedestal table to the right of the dead man. Never had the place witnessed such a riot of colours. Contrasting with the surrounding half-darkness, the clown seemed to glow from within. Ambroise changed into his suit and went to fetch the deceased's daughters. They were unable to hold back their tears on seeing their father in his luminous costume. Tears which Ambroise welcomed as the reward for a job well done. The two women thanked him profusely. 'It's the image we wanted to remember him by, you understand,' explained the eldest. 'A beautiful image,' agreed Ambroise. Before he left, he gazed at the dead man one last time. A dead man who was entering the hereafter with a great big smile.

17

Beth pounced on her grandson when he came home from work before he had even taken off his coat.

'He likes it, Ambroise!' she exclaimed ecstatically. 'Just think, he likes it!'

'What does he like?'

'*Far breton*, he likes *far breton*!'

'Who does?'

'The mog, he likes *far breton*. He loves it!'

Ambroise smiled. She hadn't said 'your' mog, but 'the' mog, a sign that she was beginning to accept him. Since the tom had been sharing their apartment, he had refused to be stroked and spent most of his time hiding under the furniture. As for food, he contented himself with gobbling a handful of pellets. Not even the can of tuna that Ambroise had opened the previous day had been much of a success. After lapping up some of the liquid, the cat had disdainfully ignored the luxury food. Beth presented her grandson with the tray on which nothing remained but a forlorn chunk eaten away on all sides.

'Look at this! I left it to cool on the kitchen table as I always do. It was the noise that alerted me. The mog had gone crazy. Never seen anything like it. He was wolfing down great mouthfuls, without stopping for breath, prunes and all. I took it away from him in the end, otherwise he'd have polished off the whole thing. Come and see him,' she said, dragging Ambroise into the living room.

Stretched out on the sofa, the tom was snoring, exposing his bloated belly for all to see. After watching him for a few moments, Beth tiptoed out, pulling Ambroise after her. The woman who not so long ago would have chased the animal off the soft cushions with a broom now showed herself to be as attentive as could be.

'He's been like that for nearly two hours. Let's leave him to sleep, shall we? *Far breton* is heavy on the stomach. You have to allow time to digest. Nature sometimes rebels against such an intrusion.'

Half an hour later, the animal was still asleep between Ambroise and Beth who were snacking from a TV tray. The doorbell rang just as the geeky face of news anchorman David Pujadas filled the screen. The tom opened his good eye, stretched voluptuously and then let himself drop to the floor to go in search of a drink of water. Ambroise and Beth looked at each other and sighed. The distinctive way of pressing the bell left no doubt as to the tiresome visitor's identity. Each ring was so brief that it could have been imagined.

'This is the second time she's come this week,' groaned Ambroise, heaving himself up from the sofa.

'What can I do?' replied his grandmother, making her way resignedly to the door while he fled to his room.

Odile Chambon stood there in her pink slippers, stamping her feet impatiently on the doormat. The heiress to the Chambon plant nurseries, whose famous slogan *Du Beau, du Bon, du Chambon* had been plastered over the region's advertising hoardings in the 1970s, lived on the ground floor and, at a loss as to how to spend her time, over the years had ended up taking on the role of concierge. The building's residents tolerated this usurpation with kindness, particularly because she did this for nothing, her only aim being to occupy her spare time. She watched over everything, kept an eye on all the comings and goings, managed the rubbish bins, distributed the post, took messages if necessary, and sent Jehovah's Witnesses and other door-to-door peddlers of religion packing with a flea in their ear. Beth tried to block the doorway to avoid the intrusion of the concierge into the apartment. It was hard to fathom the age of this beanpole of a woman, all elbows and knees. She had a ghostly pallor from spending her days reading, never venturing out into the fresh air. Her auburn hair emphasized her translucent complexion even more. Odile Chambon worshipped Ambroise Larnier and never missed an opportunity to come and inhale him and devour him with her eyes, even if only for a few moments. Any excuse would do. She'd borrow a litre of milk one day, return the milk owed the next, come to inform them that the electricity man had been to read the meter, that the Jeandrons' apartment on the second floor was being refurbished and there might be some noise during the day. Since this coming Thursday was a public holiday, the bins wouldn't be emptied until Friday. Every 7 December, she came to wish Ambroise happy St Ambrose's day, and every 4 July, to wish Beth happy St Elisabeth's day. At Christmas, a little gift, at Easter, a chocolate egg, and for Valentine's Day, it wasn't unusual to find a scented card among the post. The spinster had found her Prince Charming, and this prince, whether he liked it or not, was called Ambroise Larnier.

'Isn't Ambroise home?' inquired the lovelorn damsel. 'I cut out this article from the latest *Science and Life* magazine. It's an interview with his father about hospital-acquired infections.'

'I'll give it to him when he comes out of the shower. Thank you, Odile.'

'Oh, isn't he cute?' gasped Du-Beau-du-Bon-du-Chambon.

Beth thought for a moment that the exclamation was prompted by her grandson before realizing that it was addressed to the tomcat who was ambling nonchalantly along the passage towards them. Flabbergasted, Beth watched the creature come and rub its flanks against the concierge's bony calves, purring with pleasure, winding sinuously around her in increasingly tight figures of eight, then rolling over onto the mat to offer his belly for stroking. Odile Chambon crouched down to grab the cat who not only allowed himself to be caught without spitting, but purred even louder as she caressed him. Beth couldn't believe her eyes. This animal, who until now had refused all contact and was as sociable as a lamp post, was literally swooning in ecstasy as the concierge's fingers kneaded his ginger fur. His good eye bored into his benefactress, exuding affection, while his stumpy tail waved in all directions.

'What do you call your lovely pussycat?' asked Odile, scratching the neck of the mog who drooled with delight.

'We don't call him anything,' confessed Beth, suddenly realizing that she and her grandson hadn't taken the trouble to give the creature a name. 'And anyway, it's not my pussycat, it's Ambroise's,' she added.

These words had such an effect on Odile Chambon that she closed her eyes. For a few seconds, it was no longer a cat she was holding, but the young man himself, bestowing countless caresses on him.

The bedroom door opened and Ambroise dashed into the bathroom, yelling a 'Hello, Odile' that sounded as neutral as possible. Don't give her anything to latch onto, keep a safe distance at all costs so as not to raise any futile hopes. A lingering look, a cheerful tone, the ghost of a smile, an involuntary touch could become chinks into which Odile Chambon might slip without restraint. Generally when she came by, Ambroise tried to keep out of sight, or at least to ignore her, but it seemed that despite all his attempts to cool her ardour, on the contrary they only increased her attraction to him.

'Isn't he beautiful?' intoned the spinster, devouring with her eyes the place where Ambroise had appeared a second earlier.

This time, there was no doubt in Beth's mind as to whom the compliment was addressed.

She took advantage of Odile Chambon's visit to ask her to take the rubbish down and put it in the bin outside, as she often did. Ambroise forgot half the time and it saved her wearing her legs out going down and up the three flights of stairs. She snatched back the cat, who yowled with annoyance, and plonked the bin bag in the concierge's arms, then closed the door with a 'Good night, Odile', which echoed with a finality in the stairwell. Du-Beau-du-Bon-du-Chambon stroked the bin bag a couple of times before coming back down to earth and returning to her apartment with the fleeting image of the young Ambroise Larnier still etched on her mind.

18

The brass name plate gleamed brightly.

DR FRANÇOIS-XAVIER GERVAISE,
FORMER PARIS HOSPITALS RESIDENT,
NEUROLOGIST

An aristocratic first name followed by a surname from a Zola novel with a whiff of the farmyard. *Enter without ringing the bell*. Like a brain tumour, thought Manelle with a shudder. The secretary, with her immaculate chignon, grabbed Samuel's file and health insurance card and invited them to take a seat in the waiting room. The room exuded an overpowering odour of fresh paint. They sat down on the leatherette chairs with chrome armrests. Everything smelled new, except the pile of tatty magazines scattered on the low table. Magazines with crumpled pages, dog-eared, scrunched by the nervous fingers of anxious patients. A woman sat in one corner of the room knitting while she waited. Completely absorbed, she crossed and uncrossed her needles with the energy of a sword-fighter. Manelle patted Samuel's hand and gave him a reassuring smile. The door at the back of the room opened, and two men stood framed in the doorway. One tall and thin, the other short and stout with a sickly pallor. 'Madame Maillard, I'm returning your husband to you, he's all yours,' boomed the taller man, shaking the hand of the one with the ashen face. Doctor François-Xavier Gervaise vanished for five long minutes and then reappeared. 'It's our turn,' he said, inviting Samuel and Manelle into his sorcerer's den. He looks like a specialist, thought Manelle. A receding hairline with a shiny forehead that looked as if it had been polished, manicured hands, clean-shaven, dazzlingly white teeth – everything about him exuded hygiene and meticulousness. On the desk, a skull split open like a walnut revealed the whitish convolutions of two plastic hemispheres. 'So, what brings us here today?' asked the man of science in an artificially jovial tone. You know very well what brings us, thought Manelle, spotting the images of Samuel's brain Sellotaped to the light panel on the wall. Faced with the old man's silence and the young woman's disapproving expression, the doctor cleared his throat, embarrassed, polished the lenses of his glasses with a cloth, perused his patient's file for a few moments, then began again.

'Well, yes, Monsieur Dinsky, your brain scan appears to show a tumour mass that cannot be ignored.'

Manelle could read him like an open book. It was clear that the specialist was extremely worried about Samuel Dinsky and his tumour mass that could not be ignored.

'Appears to show or shows?' asked Samuel.

'Monsieur Dinsky, to be completely honest with you, you have a progressive cerebral tumour, which is generally known as glioblastoma multiforme or GBM.'

The doctor blurted out the words in one go, as if spitting out an annoying gob of phlegm. Glioblastoma multiforme, the name of the killer. A name redolent of metastases, thought Manelle.

'Is it operable?' she asked.

The man of science squirmed in his chair. These two with their point-blank questions were screwing up the conversation he'd planned. They were jumping the gun, sweeping aside the usual protocol. Of course the nasty thing wasn't operable, but he had to inform them according to the rules, sugar-coat the bad news with platitudes, soothe the patient's morale with a heavy dose of anaesthetic before telling him that he was fucked, totally fucked. The specialist tried to take things in hand and follow the recommended *modus operandi* for informing the condemned patient of their diagnosis.

'Naturally we can't deny the seriousness of the pathology Monsieur Dinsky is suffering from, and besides, we need to carry out further tests but there is still—'

'Is it operable, Doctor?' repeated Manelle, squeezing Samuel's hand.

'To tell you the truth, no,' said the exasperated specialist. 'In addition to the non-negligible progress of the glioblastoma, this type of invasive tumour characteristically penetrates the surrounding area and tends to erode the boundaries between the tumour tissue and healthy tissue, which makes it impossible to remove the growth through surgery.'

'What is going to happen, Doctor?' fretted Samuel, without letting go of Manelle's hand.

François-Xavier Gervaise grabbed his pen and

gently tapped the plastic brain nestled in the artificial skull.

'If the tumour had developed here, in the anterior part of the frontal lobe, psychological disorders would already have appeared. In the posterior section, you would have suffered convulsions similar to epileptic fits. In our case, given its location, we can say that the effects should be confined to disruption of the senses – taste, smell and vision. And, of course, increasingly persistent headaches caused by the increased intracranial pressure, but we should be able to control that with appropriate palliative treatment.'

François-Xavier Gervaise straightened up, relieved to have been able to place his 'in our case', a key empathetic formula that reinforced the doctor–disease–patient relationship. Manelle had great difficulty banishing from her thoughts the repulsive image of a giant voracious tick latched onto Samuel's brain and growing fat at the expense of its host.

'How long, Doctor?' asked the old man, who had slumped in his chair.

Relieved to get off so lightly, the specialist announced clearly, 'About five centimetres.'

'No, how long does he have left to live, Doctor?' Manelle translated, infuriated.

The doctor's Adam's apple yo-yoed up and down. The dreaded question. Making medicine, in the space of a calculation, an exact science. Debit, credit, balance. The balance of a life.

'Given the size of the tumour and the speed of its progression, I'd say maximum a year.'

'I'm sorry to press you, but what I'm interested in is the minimum,' said Samuel.

'Three months, at worst,' the specialist eventually admitted.

Ninety days. The time it took a parasite to kill its host. The equivalent of a season. The time for an embryo to become a foetus. The length of a short-stay visa. More than enough for a voyage around the world with Jules Verne. They paid and left without a word, holding on to each other. To see them, it was hard to tell whether the old man was supporting the young woman or she was supporting him. On leaving the consulting room, with its smell of fresh paint and its air conditioning, Samuel couldn't help glancing at the clock on the wall behind the secretary. For a moment he was convinced that the seconds were ticking by much faster than when they had arrived. The warmth and noise of life outside engulfed them.

19

'You haven't forgotten that I'm with the living this evening, have you?' yelled Ambroise from the bathroom.

'No, I haven't forgotten, and I've even made you a prune *far breton*. It's still warm,' replied Beth.

'You're a real grandmother to me,' teased Ambroise as he stepped into the shower.

He particularly savoured that moment under the purifying water when he returned from the world of the dead. He'd had an exhausting day. Six customers including one who'd committed suicide with a shotgun, which involved a partial maxillo-facial reconstruction. Nearly thirty minutes of wax modelling to achieve an acceptable result. Ambroise let the scalding jet pound his aching back, and closed his eyes. Images of his work rarely haunted him, even though, naturally, he couldn't prevent some of them from lodging in his mind. He knew they were there, those grisly visions, stored somewhere in a corner of his brain, ready to jump out of the horror chest when sparked off by a memory. He knew from having tried in the early days of his career that attempting to banish them was impossible. So he took ownership of them, aware of their presence in the way a healthy carrier can be aware of the disease they are hosting. He soaped and rinsed himself abundantly, then shook his mop of black curls and got dressed. Jeans, T-shirt, hoodie and a pair of Redskins. Colourful, comfortable clothes, a far cry from the black and white costume of the doctor to the dead.

'And you, don't forget *Ding ding* before you go,' Beth intercepted him as he came out of the bathroom, holding out the little metal box containing the kit.

'Yes, chief. And, as they say, left leg Tuesday . . .'

'. . . good news day,' said Beth with a smile.

Ambroise had already removed the metal lid. With a few deft movements, he drew the liquid into the syringe and tapped it with his index finger, then he disinfected the upper part of his grandmother's thigh with a wad of cotton wool soaked in alcohol before jabbing in the needle. Elisabeth Larnier had suffered from diabetes for more than twenty years and needed a daily insulin injection. As a child, whenever he had the opportunity, Ambroise liked to help Beth administer her shot. The little fellow obeyed his grandmother's orders like an operating-theatre nurse. She had taught him how to remove the packaging from the single-dose syringe, clean the skin around the injection site, pierce the rubber stopper and draw the colourless liquid into the syringe from the vial, and to gently push in the plunger to clear any air bubbles. Each time, she would chant him her made-up rhyme, *Ding, ding, insulin*. 'So that you know where to inject,' she told him softly. He learned the words by heart and recited them every night in bed, as if saying a prayer, at the time when he knew Beth would be injecting herself and wincing.

> *Right arm Monday, fun day*
> *Left leg Tuesday, good news day*
> *Right buttock Wednesday, friends' day*
> *Left arm Thursday, the worst day*

Right leg Friday, don't cry day
Left buttock Saturday, natter day,
And last is Sunday, stomach day!

One Sunday evening, his grandmother had asked him to perform the operation from beginning to end. Aged all of twelve, utterly focused and without trembling, he had pushed the needle into Beth's abdomen, surprised to feel the ease with which the needle went into the soft flesh. 'Not bad at all. You do it a lot better than I do,' she'd congratulated him, ruffling his hair. She'd left him to dispose of the needle in the plastic box. 'Never forget to do that, Ambroise,' she liked to remind him. 'A needle left lying around always finds a finger to prick.'

When he had come to live with her almost ten years later, she found it natural to entrust him with this daily task. So, every evening, with the same tenderness, even though he'd repeated those gestures a thousand times, Ambroise administered the old woman's dose of insulin.

'You're my favourite junkie,' he'd tease, pulling Beth's skirt back down.

'If only you would bring one of them home,' she sighed as Ambroise put the kit away.

'A junkie?' he asked, even though he knew very well what Beth meant.

'No, you idiot. One of your "living", as you call them.'

'The last one I brought home fell in love with your *kouign-amann* and she'd have ended up obese if we'd stayed together,' replied Ambroise. 'I left her for her own good. Don't wait up for me,' he added, 'I won't be back before two or three o'clock in the morning. I'm not working tomorrow and it'll do me good to hang out with young people. I can't stand living with an old woman any more,' he went on, planting a kiss on Beth's forehead as he walked past, while she gave him her prize pout as she placed the dish containing the *far breton* in his hands.

20

The parish hall where the company was performing was thirty minutes away. Ambroise parked his car in the adjacent car park and took the little case from behind the passenger seat. Even though the make-up products used for the living were absolutely identical to those he used for his habitual patients, he had still bought duplicate supplies of all the products and a vanity case to put them in covered in a brightly coloured fabric, very different from the dark leather of his embalmer's cases. And if he was missing a blusher, a jar of gel or rice powder, it would never have occurred to him to go and borrow the missing item from the cosmetics bag of the dead. It was a rule he never broke. He would not mix the two worlds between which he constantly oscillated, even though for him, the one couldn't exist without the other. He went over to Jean-Louis, the director, who was smoking a cigarette in the car park with Xavier and Sandrine, two of the actors.

'How is it?' asked Ambroise as he greeted them all with kisses.

'Five-star luxury, my lord,' replied the director. 'Toilets the size of Versailles where you'll be able to powder and primp these ladies and gentlemen without being cramped. You even have a wall mirror. The actors find the stage a little small, but you know what they're like, never satisfied,' he joked, clapping Xavier on the back.

The company never really knew what kind of theatre they would be performing in. A church hall, like this evening, a cinema, a gym, a library, a covered school playground or, more rarely, a real theatre. Adjusting to the venue and transforming it as far as was possible was the challenge every time. Exactly as for a home procedure, thought Ambroise. A body lying on the floor of a tiny bedroom, a deceased person lying on an old door on trestles in the middle of a garage, a family that categorically refuses to leave the room during the process, relatives even more silent than the body, others who won't stop talking, not to mention the general condition of the body which often brings its share of surprises – there was never a dull day for the embalmer. Ambroise walked into the hall where stage-hands and actors were rushing around. He shook hands, kissed cheeks and gave hugs. Whenever he was with the living, he had the pleasurable feeling of belonging to a lovely big family whose members came from all different walks of life. Jean-Louis was a dentist, Xavier a teacher, Sandrine worked in a supermarket, Yves was a painter, Louise a lifeguard, Mireille a secretary. And so on with all the fifteen enthusiasts who made up the amateur dramatics company.

Ambroise had discovered them two years earlier through an ad by the reception desk at his hair salon. *The Fountain Players amateur theatre company are looking for a volunteer make-up girl for their forthcoming season and longer if the fit is right. GSOH essential.* Even though he was the wrong gender, the GSOH had decided him to try his luck. They'd taken to him immediately. Especially the women, who were only too happy to put their faces in the hands of this cute young Apollo who wielded brushes, eyeshadow, mascara and lipstick like a real pro.

'Larnier? Are you related to the Nobel laureate?' they'd asked him the first evening.

'Vaguely,' he'd replied evasively. 'He's a very distant relative.'

And it wasn't long before they asked the question he feared most:

'What's your day job?'

Instead of lying, when Ambroise was asked this question he would sometimes use an expression of the Master's: 'I spend my days among the dead.' Or, if he was in a jocular mood, he'd say restorer, which invariably led to a misunderstanding. Here in town? Yes, here and around the region. Which museum? Ah, but I didn't say I worked for a museum, he would reply. But you said you're a restorer. Do you restore paintings or what? I sometimes carry out restorations but not in connection with a museum. The conversation could go on for ages. You restore paintings? No, but you're getting warm, Ambroise would encourage. Furniture? No. Buildings? No closer. A guessing game that he spun out as he pleased, until he uttered the two words which instead of stemming the tide of curiosity, had the effect of unleashing a new avalanche of questions: body restorer. With the amateur dramatics company, he'd had to lie: honesty would have certainly resulted in his being thrown out. It was hard to get people who were about to entrust their faces to your hands to accept that those same hands had been messing around with corpses all day.

'I work for a company that collects infectious medical waste from hospitals, clinics and labs. Not very exciting but a guy has to make a living.'

Medical waste collector. They'd swallowed the lie easily. Ambroise hadn't even needed to show them the sunshine yellow bins with clinical waste stickers he kept in his van for disposal of the day's waste.

Less than an hour before curtain-up, the company was in a flurry of excitement. While the stagehands finished assembling the mobile panels that formed the set, Ambroise was setting up in the toilets. Jean-Louis hadn't been kidding. They were spacious with a huge wall mirror above the washbasins. He opened the vanity case and laid out the array of brushes and crayons. Louise, who'd just slipped on her costume, was the first to be made up. The company had been touring the new play around the region for nearly three months now, and had a well-oiled routine. Later, Ambroise would sneak into the back of the hall to enjoy the play among the audience. Afterwards, once the scenery had been stashed away in the two vans and the projectors put away in the cases, he would join the others for the post-mortem amid joking and laughter, over a meal of salads, cold meats, cheese and cakes which they'd all brought. But the most intense moment for Ambroise was the one when the actors came one by one to offer him their faces to be made up. Painting the living in the evenings after applying cosmetics to the dead all day was the best way of reminding himself that life could be something other than a succession of dead bodies and grieving families. Seeing moist flesh again, running his hands over warm, supple skin, feeling eyelids fluttering beneath his fingertips, massaging mobile faces and chatting re-energized him. A profusion of life, such a far cry from the silence of inert bodies. As if by chance, six corpses had passed through his hands that day, and that evening, six living actors were waiting for him in make-up. The perfect balance.

'I'm knackered,' gasped Louise, slumping down on the chair. 'I don't know what got into the kids today at the pool, but they killed me. I look half dead, what a sight.'

'No, beauty,' retorted Ambroise drawing her hair back into a crude bun while he did her make-up. 'I promise you your face is nothing like that of a corpse,' he reassured her with a smile.

21

'Can you pop in for a minute, Ambroise my boy?'

Ambroise smiled. Bourdin's questions often sounded like commands, and this was a summons to come into the office immediately. And when Roland Bourdin said 'Ambroise my boy', he could expect anything. 'For worse or for worse,' as Beth would have said. About to leave to go to a client some distance away, Ambroise made a detour via head office. He parked at the rear and went into the vast hangar where the company's equipment and vehicles were kept, entering via the showroom. The atmosphere was conducive to contemplation and remembrance. Crystal-clear water cascaded gently to the right of the street entrance, its continual burble mingling with the music coming from speakers concealed behind the lushness of an artificial ivy. An army of crucifixes covered the left-hand wall from floor to ceiling. Hanging from the display stand next to the counter, brass inscriptions conveyed their posthumous messages: *To my husband, To our uncle, To our grandmother, To our grandfather, To my godson.* A bed of artificial wreaths was laid out either side of the central aisle. Ambroise walked past the row of coffins on show in the second room and climbed the stairs to the first-floor office. This was the world of paperwork, accounts, invoices and estimates, light years away from the hushed, orderly world downstairs. There was a smell of reheated coffee and stale tobacco. Everywhere the shelves groaned under the weight of files. Roland Bourdin tore himself away from his computer screen to come and greet him. His daughter Francine acknowledged Ambroise with a brief nod while continuing to tap at her keyboard. Over the years, she'd become the son Bourdin had never had. Short hair, always dressed in shirt and trousers, broad-shouldered, the woman everyone in the funeral world called Francis had consciously cultivated and internalized this masculinity to perfect the gender identity theft desired by her father. Bourdin invited Ambroise to sit down.

'Coffee? Francine, two coffees, please, dearest. I asked you to come in, Larnier, because there's no one else I can trust to do this job. Oh, nothing especially complicated. A body to be embalmed and repatriated from Switzerland. Eighty-two years old, less than sixty kilos. Two days for the return journey, plus three days there. Don't ask me why three days, the client is king, especially when he pays well. The deceased has no family left apart from a twin brother. He's the one who contacted us. He'll travel with you, there and back. A nice sum for the firm plus a fat bonus for you, Ambroise my boy. You haven't taken a single day off for ages. Treat it as a holiday, Larnier. A junket. Four-star hotel on the shores of Lake Geneva. And at this time of year the lakeside is quite something. I confess that if I didn't have to steer the ship, I'd have been tempted to go myself. No need to tell you that we're offering the client a turnkey service and that everything must be flawless. You leave on Monday.'

Ambroise said to himself that his boss was a master of brevity. A broad grin spread across Roland Bourdin's craggy face as he leaned towards him. 'You'll take the Vito,' he whispered magnanimously.

The Mercedes Vito, the crowning argument. Roland Bourdin's pride and joy. The most luxurious hearse in the company's fleet, with a cold storage compartment for transporting the dead and four proper seats for living passengers.

'One more thing, you have an appointment tomorrow afternoon with the deceased's brother. He wants to go over all the details of the trip with you and will pay upfront. It won't take you more than half an hour. Francine has written down the address and prepared the contract for him to sign.'

As Ambroise set off again, he realized he hadn't uttered a single word from the moment he'd set foot inside the office until he left. Pressured as he often was by Bourdin, his silence had been taken for tacit agreement. Then he thought of Beth, of her daily insulin jab, how he was going to have to abandon his grandmother for five days. Even though she still had all her marbles, increasingly she would muddle up the days, and sometimes mistake the moment when the sky takes on an evening glow for morning, confusing dusk with dawn. Forgetting an injection could have serious consequences. The Vito had four seats. That was more than were needed. He had made up his mind even before leaving behind the suburbs. Beth would come with him. Bourdin wouldn't know anything about it. He had often heard his grandmother say she dreamed of seeing the famous Geneva fountain. He was going to make her dream come true. As for the theatre, the next performance wasn't for another three weeks. And for the cat, Ambroise had a little plan.

22

Fragrant smells greeted Manelle's nostrils as she went into the apartment. An aromatic bouquet, a subtle blend of rosemary, bay leaves, onions and roast meat, was coming from the kitchen. On the last Thursday of each month, Samuel shared his meal with his home help. A meal he made it a point of honour to cook himself, and which he began several hours, even several days, in advance. When Thursday dawned, the old man was up at daybreak, lining up the utensils, taking the ingredients out of the fridge and laying everything out on the worktop. Then he bustled around amid his pots and pans concocting the dish of the day. Manelle couldn't resist the temptation to slip into the kitchen and peep inside the casserole dish. On a bed of potatoes, carrots and onions, a joint of meat was simmering over a gentle heat, exposing its golden surface. Manelle didn't bother to open the fridge. She knew that the Black Forest gateau in a sea of home-made Chantilly cream which always rounded off the monthly dinner date would be there. A dessert that she was convinced must keep Samuel busy for most of Wednesday afternoon and which had probably sapped his little remaining strength.

The disease was progressing rapidly, much too rapidly in Manelle's view. Each day the beast gained a little more ground, feeding on the old man's defenceless body. The tumour would gradually empty him of his substance until nothing remained but an emaciated wretch. Almost one month after the visit to the neurologist, he had grown even thinner. He ate less and less and sometimes vomited the little he did manage to swallow when the headaches became unbearable. Above his prominent cheekbones, his sunken eyes had lost the sparkle that used to light up his face. On Monday, Manelle had come across the old man standing stock-still in the middle of the living room, dazed, his eyes vacant, the pain having mercifully given him a moment's reprieve. A lost creature in the midst of the lull, waiting apprehensively for the return of that insatiable mistress who now shared his life. At the rate things were going, Doctor Gervaise's prognosis of three months seemed highly optimistic.

'How's my little ray of sunshine?' asked Samuel as Manelle planted a kiss in the hollow of his rough cheek. Despite the illness consuming him, he always worried about how she was. Even if increasingly his cheerful tone was feigned, his concern for her never was, and he took a genuine interest in her welfare. Had she slept well? Was she eating enough? Did she have the time to have fun, go out, see people other than old folk at the end of their lives? She reassured him, gave an evasive 'Yes, no worries,' or more often threw the question back at him. She never talked to him of her solitude filled with bland TV dinners, books avidly devoured to savour the words of others, sleepless nights dreaming of being elsewhere. After a workday spent flitting from one home to another, cleaning, tidying, ironing, scrubbing and cooking, once she finished she wanted nothing more than to get home as quickly as possible and flop on her sofabed. Even the thought of going out again was exhausting. As time went by, it felt more and more difficult to escape the life in which she had imprisoned herself. Entering into solitude the way a nun enters a religious order. That's your punishment, girl, she often told herself. A lifetime to pay for her crime. Sometimes, in the middle of the night, the little creature, bloody and shrieking, would drag her from her sleep. As if the embryo created in her adolescent womb a few years earlier and suctioned towards death by an obstetrician had never stopped growing inside her. The nineteen-year-old girl she'd been at the time had felt utterly incapable of keeping a child and the decision to have an abortion had seemed like the only option. VTP. Three ordinary-sounding letters spelling out the solution. Voluntary Termination of Pregnancy. Because that was what it was about: a lump, a cluster of insignificant cells no more desired than a malignant tumour, the result of a fling with a guy whose face she couldn't even remember, let alone his name. She'd found out too late that the choice to abort could be much worse than the gamble of having the baby. Manelle had never got over the grief of losing those few grams of life that had been torn from her.

As every last Thursday of the month, Samuel didn't wait until Manelle had finished her household chores to invite her to come and sit down at the table. They ate with the strange awkwardness that the disease, like an invasive squatter, had insidiously created between them. Silence crept in amid the discreet sounds of chewing, piled up in thick layers hardly diluted even by the driving rain beating against the kitchen window. An unbearable silence which Manelle broke before it drowned everything.

'You don't have to make a Black Forest gateau every time, you know. It really is a huge amount of work.'

For a man in your condition, she nearly added. Even unstated, the implication was there between them, hovering in the renewed silence, before Samuel broke it again.

'You've never asked me any questions about it,' he said, jerking his chin at the rich cake sitting on the table. 'In all the time I've been forcing it on you, you haven't once asked me why a Black Forest gateau and not something else. Just as you've always had the tact never to mention this,' Samuel went on, tapping the series of purple numbers tattooed on the inside of his forearm. 'They go hand in hand. I mean the cake and this number. I was twelve. There was this Black Forest gateau made by my mother, a Black Forest gateau as only she knew how to bake. I'd just taken my first bite when the men in black leather coats appeared. My last image of the world before the horror is of that gateau. Its chocolate sponge topped with Chantilly cream and sprinkled with cherries in kirsch sitting in the middle of the table, and all around, the sounds of boots, orders being barked, and screams.'

Then, and for the first time in his life, Samuel began to talk about Sobibor. It was as if the sluice gates of a giant dam had just given way. He described the survival of the frightened little animal he had become within a few weeks at the camp. The filthy work, hunger, disease, lice, beatings and death everywhere, lurking, striking blindly. As he spoke, Manelle could see the fear returning to his eyes.

'You know, Manelle, the only thing that enabled me to hold on in that hell was this gateau and the taste of that first mouthful etched on my palate and preserved like a sort of talisman. It's thanks to that memory that I held out. When I lay on my freezing bunk, shivering and starving to death, I thought about that cake. I imagined its creaminess in my mouth, the delicate crunch of the cherry, the lightness of the sponge. I dreamed it was waiting for me, fresh and soft like that first day, and that in devouring it, I would be able to bring back our life as it was before. It was there, in the middle of that nightmare, that I swore I'd become a pastry cook if I ever got out alive. For more than forty years, in the back of my shop, I made Black Forest gateaux and all sorts of cakes for my customers, in the naive and absurd belief that a person who eats cake cannot be fundamentally bad. When I returned from the camp, I convinced myself that death would never come back to toy with me, that it was weary of me and would be content, when the time came, to blow me out like the flame on a candle. I don't intend to allow death the pleasure of waltzing with me again as it did for months with the boy in hut number forty-eight in Sobibor.'

As he spoke, Samuel had picked up the envelope sitting on the kitchen dresser. He took out the file it contained and placed it in front of Manelle. She couldn't help shuddering at the sight of the word *Deliverance* printed in dark letters in the top right-hand corner of the folder. She had already heard of this association based in Switzerland that helped those opting for medically assisted suicide. An outfit which, in exchange for payment, provided a lethal cocktail to those suffering from an incurable disease who wanted to escape the suffering in which they were mired. She carefully read the pastel-coloured brochure vaunting the association's merits. There were photos of bedridden elderly people with smiling faces, in sunlit rooms. A travel agency ad for a faraway destination, thought Manelle with disgust. She couldn't suppress a shiver at the sight of the ten-page contract. It was the same sort of contract that she'd had to sign for the termination. Everything seemed to have been meticulously planned. The date and time of the appointment for the compulsory medical check-up by the doctor whose job was to ascertain the applicant's initial condition, the precise address of the apartment where the procedure would take place, the detailed composition of the lethal potion, the name and photo of the accompanying person. The medical records were attached. Samuel had scrawled his initials at the bottom of each page. A marriage contract with the Grim Reaper, thought Manelle, closing the file.

'Blow out the flame, that's all I ask,' argued Samuel. 'They do that very well, you know. I'm waiting for the owner of the funeral directors I contacted for the journey. Everything is paid for already. Deliverance is in Morges, on the shore of Lake Geneva. The anteroom to heaven,' he joked, without much conviction. 'We leave next Monday. It will only take a few days. I have no family left, no one other than you, and I'd really like to have you beside me. Don't see this request as the whim of a mad old man. I'm very conscious that what I am asking you to do goes far beyond the call of duty and I would understand if you said no, but you are the only person in the world I can ask to do this.'

Manelle had stood up. The embryo was screaming inside her.

'Once, I assisted death, so please don't ask me to be its accomplice a second time. My job is to help people to live, not to die,' she burst out, her vision blurred by tears, before fleeing the apartment.

23

Beautiful was the first word that came into Ambroise's head at the sight of the young woman who opened the door to him, just before she turned into a shrew.

'I know why you're here and I hope you're proud of what you do. It's disgusting, do you hear me, disgusting! It's aiding and abetting murder, there's no other word for it. Aiding and abetting murder, that's what it is. I wonder how you can face yourself in the mirror each morning. You ought to be ashamed of yourself. Ashamed.'

The girl had spat those last words in his face and banged into him as she left, her eyes full of tears. A fragrance of vanilla floated in her wake. Her footsteps echoed on the glistening pavement as she ran through the rain to her car. It took her two attempts to start up her ancient Polo, which finally spluttered into life. She pulled away from the kerb with a screech of tyres and shot off in a cloud of grey fumes. Ambroise stood there speechless for a few moments. He had to convince himself that he hadn't imagined the fleeting but nevertheless wonderful apparition he had just witnessed. He had to persuade himself that the curly jet-black hair, the magnificent dark eyes that had looked daggers at him, the slender chest that heaved beneath the pale green overall as she spoke, the voice which, he was certain, must be soft when it wasn't distorted by anger, and the pretty mouth from which the words had gushed were real. *Beautiful.* Despite the volley of hysterical abuse he'd just received, the adjective continued to spin inside Ambroise's head. Never had that epithet seemed to describe someone so aptly. Ambroise had already encountered strange reactions to embalming from the relatives of a deceased person, had sometimes met with defiance, embarrassment or lack of comprehension, but never had he been the butt of such venom.

The male voice inviting him to come in jolted him

out of his reverie. Shuffling slowly down the passageway, the old man coming to greet him was short and frail-looking. Barely fifty-five kilos and just over one metre sixty, Ambroise reckoned. Despite the suffocating heat in the place, he was wrapped up in a thick dressing gown and had wound a woollen scarf around his neck. The deep crow's feet around his eyes gave his face a friendly expression, despite his pallor. Ill, thought Ambroise as he shook the old man's dry, warm hand.

'Are you the gentleman from the funeral directors? I apologize for that little scene at the door,' stammered the old man. 'It's all my fault. You must forgive Manelle, she's such an impulsive young woman.'

Manelle. The two syllables sounded like music to Ambroise's ears. He wondered how a person could harbour such violence when they had such a sweet name. The old man showed Ambroise into the sitting room. Heavy curtains absorbed the sunlight, plunging the room into half-darkness.

'I'm sorry, but daylight makes my head ache,' he apologized as he switched on the centre light. 'Do sit down, Monsieur . . . ?'

'Larnier, Ambroise Larnier,' replied Ambroise, sinking into a soft armchair.

'Good. Now I believe Monsieur Bourdin has told you why I have requested your company's services?'

'Yes. It is a matter of performing the procedure and repatriating your twin brother's body from Switzerland to France, is that correct?'

'Absolutely. And did he inform you that I would be travelling with you on the way there and on the way back?'

'He did. That won't be a problem, our hearses have extremely comfortable passenger seats.'

'Very good, perfect. I have the cheque ready for you. Monsieur Bourdin and I agreed on an advance but I'd rather pay the full amount now. The hotel is already booked, too. The Regent, for four nights.'

Ambroise produced the contract which Samuel hastily signed. Ambroise cleared his throat, embarrassed.

'It doesn't say so in the document but we will be accompanied by a family support volunteer.'

Beth had made no secret of her excitement at the idea of the trip. This expedition to Switzerland had set her talking non-stop about the country. The water fountain, chocolate, fondue, perch fillets, potato rösti, referendums, finance. Ambroise had had to dampen her enthusiasm by reminding her that the initial purpose of this trip was to transport a cadaver and not, as she suggested, to go and lay a wreath in front of the Hôtel de la Paix in Geneva where the pop singer Mike Brant had tried to commit suicide the first time, in 1974. He had primed her on the improvised role of family support volunteer that she was going to be playing. Knowing his grandmother, he had stressed that he expected her to conduct herself with moderation. 'Above all, don't overdo it,' he had said. 'Respectful silence will be the most appropriate. And you don't need to say that you're my grandmother. That won't look very professional.' Ambroise had repeated his story countless times, even saying it aloud in front of the bathroom mirror. Even so, he felt his cheeks turning red and his ears burning as he gave Samuel Dinsky his spiel. He'd never been good at lying and doing so was torture.

'Don't worry, she won't be involved in the process at all. Her role is purely to be there to offer support. I hope you don't object. Naturally, Bourdin will cover all her expenses,' concluded Ambroise, relieved to have reached the end of his fib.

'No problem,' retorted the old man. 'On the contrary, I'm reassured by your professionalism. I'll book an extra room for this person, at my expense. Oh yes,

I insist. You have probably already eaten, but allow me to offer you a slice of Black Forest.'

Ambroise, who hadn't eaten a thing since breakfast, accepted with pleasure. He liked this man. Despite his obvious state of frailty, he exuded a strange serenity. Samuel came back from the kitchen with a huge piece of gateau, which he held out to Ambroise. A quarter of an hour later, his stomach full, he took leave of the old man, saying to himself that this fellow was like his cake: rich and generous.

24

The windscreen wipers were of little use against the torrential rain. Manelle honked furiously at the car in front of her when the lights changed to green. *What are you waiting for? The rain to stop?* Since she'd left Samuel and bumped into the death merchant on his doorstep, Manelle had been unable to calm down. The old man had re-opened her wound, unlocking the buried memories that now seeped out like impure blood. She recalled the radiant sunshine that day, the brilliant whiteness of the buildings, the glazed doors that had slid noiselessly shut behind her, the wall fountain where clear water had cascaded with a hideous gurgling. The lift had whisked her down to the basement, far from the sunlit, flower-filled rooms of the first floor where babies with pink or blue wristbands burbled contentedly in the arms of their elated mothers. The only light flooding the room where she had been taken came from neon tubes. It was not a place where you lingered, but a place where you arrived surreptitiously and left in a daze, with a yawning emptiness in the middle of your body. Despite the local anaesthetic, she'd shuddered when the speculum had slid inside her. She'd closed her eyes when the tube attached to the electric pump sucked out the fruit of her womb until nothing was left, just an empty space where future remorse could nest. It had taken the surgeon less than ten minutes to carry out the procedure, for a fixed price of four hundred and thirty-seven euros and three cents. A cut-price death, one hundred per cent covered by the healthcare system. As she left the hospital, she had seen another girl. Robotic walk and eyes filled with repugnance, a reflection of herself.

As the rain beat down even more violently, Manelle promised herself that to make up for not having been able to give life, she would do her utmost to fight death.

25

Ambroise had slept badly. Beth's excitement was contagious and he hadn't managed to drop off until the early hours, just before his grandmother's ancient clock woke the entire building, its bells chiming loudly on the dot of six thirty. Even the cold shower he forced himself to take wasn't enough to drag him out of his comatose state. It was Beth's luggage that finally woke him up when he stubbed the big toe of his left foot on the enormous metal trunk sitting in the middle of the passage. He hobbled into the kitchen emitting a stream of curses.

'What's that thing?' groaned Ambroise, vigorously rubbing his throbbing toe.

'Your grandfather's old army trunk.'

'Couldn't you find anything smaller? We're not going on a Nile cruise.'

'I've never found anything better for packing my clothes in. At least my dresses and coats don't come out all crumpled when I travel. Granted, it's a bit heavy, but suitcases nowadays are too flimsy,' Beth replied. 'And we may not be off on a Nile cruise, but how does one know what to wear in Switzerland at this time of the year? Hot? Cold? Everything's neutral there, even the weather.'

Pleased with her definition of the Swiss climate, Beth opened the door of the oven, which was full on, and took out the twenty perfectly golden *kouignettes* – mini *kouign-amanns*. She immediately put in a second batch. The aroma of butter cooking filled the entire apartment. Ambroise nibbled at his three crispbreads without much appetite. Sitting on the windowsill, the mog, busy washing himself, drank in the first rays of sunshine. The previous day, Ambroise had taken his courage in both hands and gone down to talk to Odile Chambon who had almost fainted at the sight of the love of her life standing on her doorstep in the flesh. Don't go in, whatever you do, don't go in, Ambroise had said over and over to himself as he rang the bell. Just 'Hello, Odile, could you look after the cat for a few days? Yes? Thank you. Goodbye.' But while the injunction not to enter a minefield was going round and round in his head, Du-Beau-du-Bon-du-Chambon had grabbed his arm and pulled him into her lair. Tea? Coffee? Beer? Champagne? Do sit down. Don't sit down. Whatever you do, don't sit down. Coffee, please. Sugar, no sugar? 'No, no sugar,' he had stammered. The eyes of a praying mantis, she's got the eyes of a praying mantis, he thought, sitting down on the living-room sofa. Say something, say something quickly, before she eats you up.

'Autumn's come early this year, hasn't it? I see they've been doing some works in Rue de la Serpentine. The sewers, I think. Or cables. They're installing fibre optic everywhere.'

For several minutes, Ambroise made small talk, hiding behind a wall of words that made no sense. What the hell was Beth doing? They'd agreed that if he wasn't back in ten minutes, she'd come and rescue him by making up some silly excuse. The bell rang just as Ambroise ran out of steam. 'Hello, Odile. Ambroise, can you come upstairs, Monsieur Bourdin's on the phone for you,' his grandmother lied with aplomb. He apologized and took his leave. 'Is it OK for the cat?' Beth asked as they climbed up the stairs. Ambroise struck his forehead and swore. 'Shit, the cat!' In the panic, he'd completely forgotten the reason for his visit to Odile Chambon. It was Beth who finally took on the job of asking the concierge. The thought of being able to stroke Ambroise Larnier's cat for five days in a row in the absence of its master had thrilled the lovelorn lady, and she'd eagerly agreed to look after the tomcat before the words were even out of Beth's mouth.

Having finished his last crispbread, Ambroise went into the bathroom to clean his instruments. Then, after locking his suitcase, he put on his jacket to go and pick up the hearse.

'I'll be back within half an hour, make sure you're ready. Monsieur Dinsky and I arranged to leave at ten o'clock sharp. Don't forget to take the litter tray and the cat food down to Du-Beau-du-Bon-du-Chambon.'

'And the cat, don't forget the cat either,' teased Beth.

26

The Mercedes Vito stood waiting for Ambroise in the company car park. He collected the keys from the office and transferred his embalming equipment into it from his little van, and then set off. It only took a few minutes for him to acquaint himself with his new vehicle. Beth was already downstairs by the front door. Dressed in black from head to toe, the old woman looked every inch the tearful widow, apart from the basket of *kouignettes* she was holding. Ambroise had a hard job persuading her to remove the veil covering her face and the black gloves she was wearing.

'Well, are we in mourning or aren't we?' she

grumbled, putting the net veil and lace gloves away in her handbag.

'We're supporting the family, we aren't *the* family, Beth,' Ambroise explained gently, stressing the word 'the' as he went upstairs to fetch the army trunk.

They went back into the apartment to retrieve the mog, the litter tray and the cat food. Odile Chambon was waiting for them on the landing, caked in make-up, fluttering her eyelashes like mad. 'Come to Odile, my bunny rabbit', she whispered, snatching the tomcat from Ambroise's arms. 'Mama's going to look after you, you'll see. We're going to be lovely and cosy just the two of us,' she added, trying to catch Ambroise's furtive gaze with her heavily mascaraed eyes.

'I made him a *far breton*,' Beth broke in. 'I'll put it here, on the dresser. Whatever you do, don't give it all to him at once,' she added, 'because it'll take him a whole week to recover.'

On the way to Samuel Dinsky's, Beth was unable to conceal her anxiety. 'I hope it'll be all right. She called him bunny rabbit, did you hear?'

'Between you and me, he didn't seem to mind too much. You wouldn't be a little jealous, would you?'

'Jealous of what? I don't like cats, remember.'

'What if she's right? Maybe the mog is a rabbit,

with his little tail. We should try him on carrots when we get back.'

'Don't be so silly. Now, tell me what this Monsieur Dinsky's like.'

'He doesn't look in much better shape than his deceased brother, but he's charming, you'll see. And his Black Forest gateau is as good as your *kouign-amann*.'

'Do you think he'll let me sit in the front? I get car sick.'

'There are three seats in the front, in case you hadn't noticed. The seat next to the casket is for the fourth pallbearer when there's a funeral.'

The gate was open. Ambroise parked the hearse in the courtyard in front of the house and asked Beth to wait in the vehicle. Samuel Dinsky seemed even feebler than the previous week. His frail body was lost in a suit several sizes too large for him. His sparse white hair was neatly combed. There was a streak of shaving cream on one of his cheeks. Ambroise didn't dare mention it to him. He relieved him of his luggage, a half-leather, half-canvas suitcase that was surprisingly light. Samuel Dinsky gazed for a long time around the living room he'd just exited, then inspected each room one last time, making sure the shutters were properly closed and the lights off. He locked the front door and placed the key under the pot of geraniums in the hall. He winced and had to take hold of Ambroise's arm to go down the steps. The bright daylight made his migraine ten times worse. The sun's rays pierced his retinas like white-hot needles. He turned around and creased his eyes to look at the house in which he had spent most of his life. Then the old man sat down beside Beth who had moved over onto the centre seat.

'Elisabeth,' she introduced herself, holding out her hand, 'your travel companion.'

'Delighted, madame. Samuel Dinsky at your service.'

'May I?'

Beth took a handkerchief out of her bag and started dabbing at Samuel's cheek.

'My late husband was just the same. Every single morning there was always a bit of shaving foam left on his face. And when it wasn't on his cheek, it was on the tip of his ear, his chin, or sometimes even on the end of his nose.'

'Thank you, madame.'

'Beth, call me Beth, I'd like that.'

'Thank you, Beth.'

Morges was less than six hours away, seven including stops. If all went well, Ambroise reckoned they'd reach the hotel on the shores of Lake Geneva in the afternoon. He was glad he'd opted to leave mid-morning, after rush hour and before the lunchtime crowds. They drove through the outlying suburbs and took the motorway heading north.

'Have you been doing this for long?' Samuel asked.

The question was addressed to Beth.

'What do you mean, this?' she replied.

'Volunteering. Supporting relatives.'

'Well, to be completely honest, you're my first.'

Ambroise cut short the conversation by hitting the radio button in search of frequency 107.7.

'Must we really have the radio on?' asked Beth, slightly irritated.

'I like to listen to the traffic news, so we know if there's a tailback or an accident.'

'Because your eyes aren't good enough to inform you? Some driver you are.'

Ambroise glared daggers at his grandmother who took refuge in a peeved silence. A little later, the sign 'Next exit Pont du Gard' roused Samuel from his torpor.

'Excuse me, Monsieur Larnier, but could I possibly

ask you to make a detour to view the viaduct? I haven't seen it for ages.'

'Oh yes,' gushed Beth, clapping her hands like a child who's just been promised a ride on the merry-go-round.

'Well, we've still got a long way to go and I don't want to arrive after dark.'

'It's not far out of our way. And as the family support volunteer, I think it's a lovely idea that can only do Monsieur Dinsky good.'

'Samuel, call me Samuel.'

The two of them seemed to be as thick as thieves. Outnumbered, Ambroise took exit 23 signposted Remoulins, not without darting his grandmother another glowering look. He had a nasty feeling that they were going to arrive much later than his planned time. They did not get back on the road until midday, after Samuel had gazed one last time at the ancient stone arches silhouetted against the azure sky.

27

Beth and Samuel jointly requested a first stop to answer the call of nature at kilometre ninety-six, the Montélimar South interchange. Urged on by his increasingly desperate passengers, Ambroise was forced to put his foot down on the accelerator.

'There's a storm on the way, I saw a flash of lightning,' observed Beth.

'I think I did too,' agreed Samuel.

'That's funny, there isn't a single cloud,' said Beth, pushing her face closer to the windscreen to scan the sky.

'Maybe a heat flash,' suggested Samuel.

'It's barely twenty degrees. Twenty's not very hot, not for a heat flash. And they tend to happen in the evening, heat flashes.'

Ambroise was concentrating on the road and didn't bother to explain to the two old folk that the flash hadn't come from the sky but from the fixed speed cameras that had just immortalized the moment when Roland Bourdin & Sons' hearse had reached the more-than-respectable speed of 158 kilometres per hour. He turned onto the slip road to Montélimar East services and pulled into the first available parking space. He watched with a smile as Samuel and Beth hobbled together towards the toilets. As he was getting out to stretch his legs, he spotted an apple-green car parking a hundred or so metres further up. He had noticed the same vehicle earlier, in the car park at Pont du Gard. Nothing unusual about that. But something was niggling him. You don't forget that shade of green, and he was certain he'd already seen that car somewhere before, but couldn't think where. Beth broke into his thoughts when she came back from the toilet.

'I think we've lost him,' she announced anxiously.

'What do you mean, lost him?'

'Samuel, I haven't seen him come out. He should be back already.'

'Don't move from here, whatever you do. I'll go and have a look.'

Ambroise raced across the car park and dived into the men's toilet. Given the octogenarian's frail condition, it was possible he'd been taken ill. Calling his name, Ambroise bent down to look beneath the doors of the cubicles, expecting to find a body slumped on the tiled floor. He eventually found the old man near the entrance to the shop, standing in front of the sunglasses display.

'Monsieur Dinsky, we need to get going. Is something the matter?' asked Ambroise with concern at the sight of fat tears rolling down the old man's hollow cheeks.

'I'm all right. I'll be fine. It's nothing, don't worry. Just some bad memories that caught up with me.'

Samuel seemed deeply shaken and Ambroise had to help him back to the car.

'Everything's fine,' he whispered, reassuring Beth, who had a worried frown, as he slid back in behind the wheel. He put his finger discreetly to his lips, signalling to Beth that the best thing was to keep quiet for the time being and let the old man recover from the upset. As he pulled out into the acceleration lane to merge with the flow of traffic, he glimpsed their pursuer in his rear-view mirror doing the same. Pure coincidence, he told himself, even though he had a growing sense of unease about this car that had clung to them since the start of the journey. There was only one way to find out. As he had seen countless times at the cinema, Ambroise gradually reduced his speed, going from 130 down to below 110, then he suddenly accelerated before slowing down again. In the rear-view mirror, the green car grew bigger, melted then grew bigger again as he sped up or slowed down, its driver trying to keep a distance of around a hundred metres behind the hearse. There was no doubt about it, they were being followed. What could anyone want of them to stay on their tail for so long? He had no enemies to his knowledge, had no secrets, and the same was true of his grandmother. But what about Samuel Dinsky who perhaps led a double life, in the guise of a harmless octogenarian? They had been driving for more than half an hour when once again, Beth shattered his thoughts.

'It's gone one thirty. I don't know what Samuel thinks, but maybe we could stop for a bite to eat,' she suggested.

'We'll stop once we've passed Valence,' Ambroise

reassured her. 'There's a restaurant at the next motorway services, if that suits Monsieur Dinsky.'

'What do you mean, a restaurant? Whatever next?' choked Beth. 'A picnic area will do just fine. I've prepared a picnic basket for all of us. It's also part of the family support volunteer's job to look after the wellbeing of the relatives,' she added for the benefit of her grandson, with a note of mischief in her voice.

'But perhaps Monsieur Dinsky would prefer the comfort of a restaurant to a picnic table?'

'Not at all, on the contrary. It's ages since I've eaten outdoors. And even though I no longer have much of an appetite, I'd be delighted to do justice to the food you have prepared, Beth,' Samuel complimented her.

Two against one. Once more, Ambroise had to bow to the wishes of the majority. At the sight of the sign announcing Les Fruitiers picnic area, he pulled over into the slow lane.

'That's a pretty name for a picnic spot,' gushed Beth.

At this time of year, the car park was almost empty and the few tables and benches dotted around the tired lawns after a summer of being trampled intensively were nearly all free. Ambroise parked the Vito in the shade of a tree, switched off the engine and got out. Their pursuer's green car had stopped at the entrance to the rest area, its engine ticking over. Ambroise decided to ignore it, secretly hoping that the driver would eventually tire of this stupid game of cat and mouse.

'Where did you put the basket?'

'In the box at the back.'

'What do you mean, box? What box?' groaned Ambroise, fearing he knew only too well what Beth meant.

'The chiller cabinet, is there another one? We're lucky to have a mobile refrigerator, and you'd rather I hadn't used it to keep my salads and pâtés cool?'

'I don't believe it,' exploded Ambroise, racing round to the rear of the hatchback.

To his great relief, the refrigerated compartment used for transporting corpses was empty.

'See how he fell for it. So quick to fly off the handle, my Ambroise,' she gently mocked. 'He's always been like that, ever since he was little. As innocent as a lamb. And how his gullibility used to annoy his father, even if, between you and me, I think it shows a certain magnanimity. No, you silly billy, it's all in the cool bag on the back seat.'

'You sound as though you know him well,' remarked Samuel as the two of them picked their way over the grass towards the picnic tables.

'To tell you the truth, I'm his grandmother but shush, when we're working, he prefers us to keep our relationship strictly professional.'

They chose the table with the most shade, to protect Samuel's eyes from the bright sunlight. Beth spread a large gingham tablecloth and laid the table.

'Picnic or not, we're not animals. Paper tablecloths, cardboard plates and plastic cups get blown away in the wind, make the food taste bland and ruin the wine. I've made remoulade, cucumber salad and sliced beef tomato with mozzarella,' announced Beth as she unwrapped and presented the food. 'There's duck rillettes and chicken liver pâté. For those who prefer fish, I've made a salmon terrine. All home-made. For the cheese, I thought a Pavé d'Affinois, a piece of Tomme de Savoie and a slice of Brie would do the job. And a Saint-Joseph to wash it down. A Saint-Joseph is good, isn't it? What do you say?'

Stunned at the sight of such a feast, Ambroise and Samuel didn't know what to reply.

'Look at this gorgeous weather! Autumn really is a good time to go on a journey,' said Beth, spreading a generous layer of rillettes over a hunk of bread.

'A good time to go on a journey,' echoed Samuel softly.

28

As promised, Samuel did justice to the food prepared by Beth. He ate a little of everything, even asking for a second helping of remoulade. Beth insisted he have a tiny sip of the Saint-Joseph and he eventually accepted the thimbleful she poured for him. Ambroise remained slightly aloof, and ate on his feet, watching the green car out of the corner of his eye. From this distance, all he could see of the driver was a dark shape behind the windscreen. When it was time for the cheese, Samuel had to face the fact that he had over-estimated his stomach's capacity for so much food, no matter how excellent it was. The shooting pain in his temples was worse than ever and, feeling suddenly nauseous, he excused himself and left the table to totter unsteadily to the toilet. Beth rushed to help him and offered him her arm. 'It's all right, I'm looking after him,' she yelled in the direction of her grandson as she accompanied Samuel to the toilet block thirty metres away. Ambroise nodded then immediately turned his attention to the object that was preoccupying him. The green blob on the edge of his field of vision had moved. Their pursuer's vehicle had started up and was racing across the car park. Contrary to all expectations, the car pulled up next to the Mercedes Vito with a screech of tyres. Ambroise's heart began to beat wildly. In a primitive reflex, he clenched his fists, ready to do battle. The engine spluttered twice, then stalled. Curiously, the image that the Polo and its unusual colour had so far failed to evoke, that of a furious young woman in tears barging into him after hurling copious abuse at him, was aroused by the fume-filled hiccup the car gave as it stalled. And as that same young woman got out of the car and headed towards him with a determined step, he said to himself that she was even more beautiful than he remembered. Just under one metre seventy, weighing fifty-five kilos, his trained eye told him. A light tunic, jeans, soft loafers – her clothes displayed a casualness belied by her anxious gait. She stood and looked Ambroise directly in the eyes.

'Look, knowing him as I do, I imagine he won't hear of it, but don't you think there are other alternatives to his problem than the one you are preparing to commit?'

'Ambroise. Ambroise Larnier,' he introduced himself.

She continued in the same sharp tone, ignoring his proffered hand.

'How much did he pay you for this, eh? How much? It's funny, I thought funeral directors only took care of the dead, not the living,' she sneered.

'Listen, there's no point getting all het up. We are simply carrying out Monsieur Dinsky's wishes, as we always do with our clients. I don't know what alternative you mean, but we've always worked like this and I don't see what the problem is.'

'The problem? Let me tell you what the problem is: I see an old man, not really in a condition to cope with a journey like this, a man who perhaps isn't in full possession of his faculties, encouraged in his plans by people whose prime motivation is profit, profit and nothing else.'

'Well, I grant that Monsieur Dinsky perhaps over-estimated his ability to cope with such a trip and so did we, but—'

'Overestimated his ability? Overestimated his ability? Just listen to yourself! Even without being an expert, you must know that people who are on their last legs are rarely in tip-top form.'

She had a strange way of repeating herself, which made her all the more intriguing.

'At the risk of shocking you, but it seems that everything that comes out of my mouth shocks you, it's not our job to judge the wishes of a person who is suffering. And insofar as there is nothing unusual about his request, we felt it was quite natural to agree to it. That's all.'

This was the first time that Ambroise had heard himself say such a thing. What was this smarmy, idiotic spiel he was giving her? It was good for Bourdin, not for him, but she was pushing him to the limit too, yelling at him as if he were a complete thug.

'The wishes of a person who is suffering. You make me puke with your trite little phrases.'

'Now look, Manelle—'

'Oh, so you know my name too. That takes the biscuit! Mr Undertaker knows my name.'

'I'm not an undertaker,' protested Ambroise weakly.

'Oh no, of course not. So what should I call you? Mr Fancy Funeral Director. Or what about Charon, like the ferryman who carries the souls of the dead across the River Styx on his rotten boat? Charon would suit you very well!'

Just then, Samuel, back from the toilet, sank down onto the bench, still clutching Beth's arm. The colour had returned to his cheeks, as it did after each bout of vomiting. The vice gripping his head had relaxed a little. On catching sight of his home help, the old man's face lit up with a smile.

'Have you changed your mind?' he asked eagerly, with hope in his voice.

'Even though I still think you're making a mistake, I couldn't abandon you like that,' she said, grasping his hands. 'After storming out the other day without saying goodbye, I felt ashamed. I'm happy to come with you but on one condition, Monsieur Samuel-Dinsky-who-won't-listen: that you allow me to try and persuade you to change your mind as many times as I possibly can,' she whispered in his ear.

'If that's the only price to pay for the pleasure of having you beside me, then all right, but I have a condition too.'

With these words, the old man stood up and drew Manelle to one side, out of earshot.

'I'd like all this to remain a secret between you and me for as long as possible. The young man you see over there, and a charming young man he is too, knows nothing of my plans. The official story is that we're going to Switzerland to bring home the body of my deceased twin brother. It's as simple as that.'

Manelle spluttered.

'You mean that this guy knows nothing of your intentions, nothing of Deliverance? That he has no idea of the purpose of this journey?'

'Absolutely none.'

'But why invent this story about a twin?'

'Why? Quite simply because it was much easier to lie than to tell the truth. Do you know many funeral directors who would have said, OK, we'll take you there alive and bring you home dead, no worries? Sitting in the front seat on the way there, and lying in the back on the way home. Ethically, it wouldn't be acceptable. I said to myself that once faced with the *fait accompli*, the lie would no longer matter. He'll have no option but to bring my body back so that the last of the Dinskys can be buried in the family vault. And I've paid enough for the firm that employs him to feel morally committed and for the job to be seen through to the end.'

'I don't believe it,' breathed Manelle. 'Samuel Dinsky, you are the biggest liar I know,' she scolded him affectionately, wagging her finger as if reprimanding a child.

'Who's she?' Beth asked as she packed away the remains of the meal, gauging the young woman out of the corner of her eye.

'A fairy, a demon, perhaps both, I have no idea,' Ambroise replied, disconcerted.

29

Beth fetched the thermos of coffee and the basket of *kouignettes* from the van.

'Leaving the table without having dessert is like leaving mass without taking communion,' she pronounced as she placed the caramelized pastries in the centre of the table.

Samuel waited until she had sat down again before making the introductions.

'Manelle, I have the pleasure of introducing Elisabeth, who devotes her time and expertise to supporting families—'

'Beth, you must call me Beth.'

'. . . and Ambroise, our driver, but you have already had the opportunity to become acquainted, I think.'

'You could say that,' mumbled Manelle, wringing her hands.

The young woman's sudden change in behaviour baffled Ambroise. All the aggression she had shown him a few minutes earlier seemed to have vanished as if by magic, and now she appeared visibly embarrassed.

'Manelle is the person who assists me in my day-to-day life,' Samuel went on.

'A private nurse?' asked Beth.

'Not exactly, no. Manelle is what is called a home help. She comes to the house for an hour every day to assist with the jobs my age prevents me from doing. I shan't hide the fact that she's become much more than that. She makes that hour into a celebration. And with time, I've come to see her as the granddaughter I never had. A granddaughter who'd come every day of the week to visit her grandpa, sit and chat with him, and sometimes eat with him. I have reached the point where I live only for that hour spent breathing in her presence, listening to her voice, hearing her laugh, sharing her loves and hates. So it seemed perfectly natural to me to ask her to escort me on this macabre expedition. I didn't know at the time that I would be benefiting from the presence of a companion such as you, Beth.'

Beth blushed and squirmed with delight.

'At first she got angry and refused, arguing that in my condition, such a journey was sheer madness, but it seems that now she's understood that this mission is more important to me than anything else and she finally made up her mind to join us.'

As he spoke, the old man grasped Manelle's hand. Despite his visible exhaustion, he found the strength to smile at her.

'Even though I still think that this trip is anything but sensible,' declared Manelle, giving Samuel a solemn look.

While Samuel, given his digestive problems, was naturally spared the *kouignettes*, there was no excuse for his home help. Having eaten nothing since the morning, Manelle gratefully tucked into the pastries and dipped into the basket several times. She washed them down with large gulps of coffee, raving over their taste. 'They're really very good,' she said. At that moment, Manelle Flandin, home help by profession, had just unwittingly gone over to the side of the angels in the eyes of the old woman facing her, who gazed at her fondly.

When it was time to leave, Manelle insisted on Samuel going in her car. They were still nearly four hours away from Morges. Four hours, the only and last chance for her to try and talk the old man out of his morbid plan. The Polo had other ideas. When Manelle switched on the ignition, the engine spluttered and wheezed then died completely amid the smell of oil and petrol fumes. Manelle thumped the steering wheel several times and swore.

'Shit, I don't believe it. This would have to happen now. It's not true, dammit!'

'Don't worry, Manelle, it's only a car,' Samuel consoled her from the passenger seat.

'But that's not the problem, don't you understand?' she snapped, trying the ignition again.

'Stop, there's no point, the engine's dead,' decreed Ambroise.

The large pool of coolant spreading beneath the car was clear enough evidence of the seriousness of the breakdown.

'And it's a mortician who's telling me it's dead,' Manelle burst out with a hysterical laugh. She laid her head on the wheel, groaning. 'What a pain in the arse.'

All the hopes that the prospect of a lengthy tête-àtête with Samuel had aroused in her were suddenly shattered.

'Look, if you don't mind leaving your car in the car park, we can easily all fit into the hear . . . into the Vito,' Ambroise volunteered. 'And we'll get a tow truck to come out to your car on the way back. We'll find a solution.'

Yes, and on the way back there'll only be three of us, if you reckon that the dead don't count. We'll have plenty of room with just three of us, she felt like screaming in the face of this angelic-looking guy who always seemed even-tempered, whatever happened. Beaten, Manelle had to face facts: she had no option but to accept Ambroise's offer. She opened the boot and took out her little overnight bag in which she'd flung a few random items of clothing before leaving, locked the car and walked over to the hearse, flanked by the two octogenarians.

Ambroise unfolded the jump seat at the rear. Once again, he was flouting the regulations of Roland Bourdin & Sons, which prohibited anyone not an employee of the company aboard its vehicles. Manelle looked with distaste at the refrigerated compartment that occupied part of the space before sitting down.

'It's the seat for the fourth pallbearer,' Beth

explained, turning around to tap Manelle's knee before helping Samuel to fasten his seat belt, only too happy to have him sitting beside her again.

They set off. The interior soon resonated with the snores of the two old people who fell asleep almost at the same time, lulled by the gentle purr of the engine and the trickle of music from the car radio. Ambroise glanced in the rear-view mirror at regular intervals, hoping to meet Manelle's eyes, but each time, she avoided his gaze. For nearly half an hour, each waited for the other to speak first. Their mutual embarrassment was palpable. Finally, it was Ambroise who took the plunge, as they were driving through Grenoble.

'Have you been working for him for long?'

'I've never really felt I work for him,' she replied. 'He makes life seem so good, so simple and sweet. He never raises his voice, he's always considerate. Increasingly I ask myself who's the employer and who's the employee. What about you, how long have you been in this profession?'

'Almost five years.'

'And why?'

'Why "why"?'

'Why the dead and not the living?'

He detected a hint of sarcasm in her voice.

'The fact is, I don't do this for the departed, but for those who are left behind. Embalming is—'

'What?'

'The art of embalming the dead.'

'Because you do that too, embalm dead people?'

'That's mainly what I do.'

'I don't believe it.' She pulled a face as if suddenly she were confronted with the most heinous villain.

'What?' said Ambroise furiously. 'You think that there are two types of people in the world, the good and the bad? Those who look after the living and those who look after the dead? Warm-blooded and cold-blooded beings? That because I treat – yes, mademoiselle, we say "treat" for embalming too – because I treat the dead, corpses, cadavers, stiffs, call it what you like, I'm no better than the maggots that invade them if I don't intervene? Oh, of course, nice little home helps like you can't understand. You're like my father, convinced you're on the side of the angels, and that the guy facing you is no good, as devoid of feeling as the bodies he treats. But it's because I'm too sensitive that I treat the dead, would you believe? I've tried the living but I can't bear their suffering. I hate seeing people die, can you believe that? And besides, let me say it again, I do it for those who are left behind, to save them from having to look death in the face in all its repugnance. So if you're asking me why I do this job, let me give you an example: because it's easier for a mother to kiss the forehead of a son who looks as if he's asleep in a peaceful eternity than to remain haunted by the image of a face ravaged by death. And if my answer isn't what you expected, I'm sorry, but that is my reply and you won't receive any other.'

Ambroise withdrew into himself, his eyes fixed on the horizon. Manelle's gaze lingered on his closed face as if seeing him for the first time. At that moment, she found him beautiful. That young man she'd judged to be smooth and transparent had just revealed facets of a character she had not suspected. Beneath his appearance of a docile wimp was a hyper-sensitive soul. The way his eyes had flashed when he flared up had entranced her.

'I apologize, I didn't mean to offend you,' she said.

'Don't worry, it's me. I shouldn't have lost my temper like that, I'm very sorry.'

Beth and Samuel put an end to this conversation by waking up. They both stretched then asked Ambroise for another toilet stop.

30

It was after five o'clock by the time they reached the Swiss border post. In his slow drawl, and somewhat intrigued by this strange crew in what appeared to be a hearse, the customs officer questioned Ambroise as to the purpose of their journey. He explained the reason for their trip, the brief stay in Morges to bring the body of Monsieur Dinsky's brother back to France.

'Do you plan to take the motorway?' asked the customs official, inspecting the windscreen for the sticker.

'No, we intend to take the main road along the lake.'

That skinflint Bourdin had been too mean to buy a motorway pass. 'Anything to declare?' asked the officer suspiciously. *A glioblastoma multiforme*, Manelle wanted to yell at him. 'No,' replied Ambroise, echoed by Beth and Samuel who energetically shook their heads from left to right in unison, which made the man even warier.

'Would you open the hatchback, please.'

Ambroise complied, not without showing his irritation. The official made him take out his cases and unwrap all his embalming equipment. His sharp eyes roved over the instruments and bottles, and inspected the pumps before he permitted Ambroise to pack up his tools again.

'May I see your ID, please?'

The guy had decided to be zealous. Beth panicked and it took her almost five minutes to find her identity card sandwiched in her purse between her social security card and her voter's card. The customs officer scrutinized the four documents.

'Monsieur . . . Dinsky, is that right? You'd better renew your ID card, Monsieur Dinsky. It expired six months ago.'

He handed everything back to Ambroise and released them, saying magnanimously, 'I'll turn a blind eye this time.'

'So much for Europe,' fumed Beth as they set off again. 'Did you see how he treated us? As if we were crooks. And that superior air of his, with his ridiculous cap. And his "I'll turn a blind eye this time", implying that next time, it'll be go straight to jail, do not pass go. For goodness' sake, where on earth are we?'

'In Switzerland, Beth, in Switzerland,' Samuel tenderly calmed her.

As Ambroise had feared, they found themselves stuck in the Geneva traffic and it took them more than twenty minutes to cross the Mont-Blanc Bridge, which gave Beth plenty of time to marvel at the giant Jet d'Eau fountain.

'All right, so their customs officers aren't very nice but you've got to admit that when it comes to building fountains, they're the best!' she announced, transfixed by the white plume rising high into the sky.

The traffic on the main road between Geneva and Morges was more fluid than anticipated and the Mercedes Vito turned into the Regent Hotel's car park shortly before seven o'clock, just as night kissed the waters of the lake. They walked into the vast lobby with its tall, ornate mirrors. The soft lighting from the high ceilings imbued the marble colonnades with warm tones. Thick carpeting muffled footsteps. The place oozed luxury. The receptionist confirmed the three reservations. Room 101 on the first floor for Samuel, 103 for Beth and 236, on the second floor, for Ambroise. Since the hotel was full, Beth invited Manelle to share her room and she accepted.

'If the rooms are as grandiose as the lobby, there's no risk of us treading on each other's toes,' joked Beth.

The porter who took their luggage up was unable to hide his surprise at Beth's military trunk. 'It must make a change from Vuitton,' she said. Manelle went with Samuel to help him settle into his room. He sank down on the edge of the bed, completely exhausted. Manelle felt his forehead. It was clammy.

'You have a temperature. Did you bring your medicine?' she asked.

'Yes, the pill organizer is in my toilet bag. I can't help wondering why I brought it. A stupid reflex.'

'Well, I'll tell you why you brought that pill organizer, Samuel Dinsky: because deep down you still have faith. Something's telling you that despite the pain, days like today are still worth living.'

'If you say so,' murmured the old man, unconvinced.

'Would you like something to eat?'

'Not hungry.'

'Then you should go to bed,' she suggested gently, holding out the two pills and a glass of water. 'You're exhausted. And we can see about having a shower tomorrow.'

Samuel was struggling to undress, so Manelle helped him remove his clothes. She did it naturally and without embarrassment. She took off his trousers, socks, shirt and vest, slid his underpants down and assisted him into his pyjamas.

'And don't take advantage of the situation,' she laughed, 'or I'll have to fight you off and rouse the entire hotel, screaming for help.'

'I know a young Apollo who would like nothing better than to rush in and save you,' teased Samuel in a tired voice.

'I prefer wealthy old men,' she whispered mischievously as she tucked him in.

'The head of the association is coming to pick me up at the hotel at ten o'clock tomorrow to take me for my medical check-up. I'm really counting on you to come with me,' pleaded Samuel, gripping Manelle's hand.

'I promise, but only because I like old men who are loaded,' she replied, kissing his forehead and slipping out before being overcome with sadness.

Manelle went into the adjacent room where she found an ecstatic Beth busy hanging up her clothes.

'Look at this! A closet you can wander around in, it's crazy!'

'It's called a walk-in wardrobe, Elisabeth.'

'Beth, please, call me Beth. I've never liked my name. Elisabeth sounds like a nun, don't you think? It's funny when you think about it: Eliza has a nice ring, it's light, airy, but as soon as you add Beth, plop, it's as if it closes up and falls to the ground. What about you? You must like your name. Manelle is so pretty.'

'Yes, except that at school, the boys had the infuriating habit of calling me Manky Manelle.'

A knock at the door interrupted the women's conversation.

'Come in.'

'Right arm Monday, fun day,' trumpeted Ambroise, walking into the room.

'I'd completely forgotten,' confessed Beth sheepishly as she went to fetch the insulin kit.

'You see, I don't only deal with old people who are dead, I also inject old people who are alive, on occasion,' Ambroise provoked Manelle as he gave his grandmother her jab.

'And what do you do with young people?' she retorted without missing a beat.

Beth couldn't help smiling at her grandson's dejected expression as he laid down his arms, defeated before the battle had even begun.

'Shall we all meet downstairs for dinner?' he suggested.

'Samuel won't be eating. I put him to bed, he was too exhausted to swallow a thing.'

'The same goes for me, children. That long journey has done me in. I think I need a good night's sleep to build up my strength for the coming days. I'm going to take the edge off my appetite with a couple of *kouignettes* then I'm going to beddy-byes and I'll be fine. Don't worry about me, you youngsters.'

'OK, I'll wait for you in the lobby, then,' Ambroise said to Manelle, before depositing a kiss on his grandmother's forehead and leaving the room.

'Is he always so considerate towards you?' asked Manelle after Ambroise had left.

'I'm not saying this because he's my grandson, but he's the sweetest boy imaginable. And when I see how seriously he takes his job, I say to myself that the dead who pass through his hands really are very fortunate.'

31

For almost a quarter of an hour, Ambroise had been studying the various menus when Manelle jolted him from his contemplation. She had made the effort to get changed. A white blouse, a midnight-blue cardigan slung over her shoulders, dark leggings and a pair of canvas trainers. A light application of eyeliner emphasized the brightness of her eyes. 'Diamonds like that don't need a setting to shine,' Beth had assured her as she put her make-up on.

'Did you want to eat here?' Ambroise asked. 'To be honest, the restaurant is a bit too stuffy for my taste and the prices are like everything else: over the top. So if you don't mind eating somewhere where you don't get to sit in a Voltaire armchair surrounded by an army of waiters ready to pander to your every wish, I saw on the map that there's a restaurant less than five hundred metres along the shore which looks rather nice. What do you think?'

'As you like. I'm not actually very hungry. Your grandmother's whatsits are wicked.'

'*Kouignettes*. They're called *kouignettes*,' Ambroise reminded her with a smile.

They stepped out into the cool evening air and ambled along the shore to the marina, which could be seen from a distance with its forest of motionless masts. Wisps of mist curled over the lake's dark waters. On the opposite shore the town of Évian's lights twinkled brightly. It's too beautiful a place to die, thought Manelle, shivering.

'Do you want my jacket?' offered Ambroise.

'No, I'm fine, thank you. And anyway, I think we're here.'

The place was both unpretentious and warm. Huge bay windows looked out over the lake. On this dead-season Monday, there was only a handful of diners and they were able to choose their table.

'What about this one?' asked Ambroise, plumping

for the one that afforded the best view over the misty expanse.

'Perfect.'

'Would you like a drink?'

'I don't think it would do me any harm.'

'Wine? A white wine?'

Ambroise ordered two glasses of chardonnay.

'I'm worried about Monsieur Dinsky,' he said after a brief silence. 'He really doesn't seem in good shape.'

'No, and it's not going to get any better,' confirmed Manelle, looking away to hide her emotion.

'What do you mean?' asked Ambroise.

She waited until the waiter had finished pouring the wine before continuing.

'Samuel has an inoperable brain tumour. He only has a few weeks left to live.'

'Shit.'

His 'shit' expressed all the sorrow in the world, and Manelle was touched to see the genuine sadness in the way Ambroise had reacted to the news.

'It won't be long before he follows his twin to the grave,' said Ambroise after a while.

'Now that could be difficult.'

'But you just said he's only got a few weeks to live.'

'True. A few weeks at best. No, when I say that could be difficult, I'm talking about his brother.'

Manelle took a sip of the fruity wine to pluck up her courage. She had promised Samuel that she would keep his secret for as long as possible but now she'd reached the end of that 'as long as possible'. She needed to talk, to share, to seek support. She couldn't cope with being the only person to carry this burden. And the man sitting opposite her at that precise moment was perhaps the most suitable person to be told the truth. A waiter came over to take their order.

'Would you give us a moment, please? Thank you,' said Ambroise, politely deflecting him.

Manelle took a deep breath before launching into her story.

'Samuel Dinsky has never had a brother, let alone a twin,' she said in a low voice.

'What do you mean, never had a brother? What about the body we're supposed to be repatriating to France?'

'It's Samuel's.'

There, she'd said it. As predicted, Ambroise took it badly. As she herself would have done in his shoes.

'Hold on, you're trying to tell me that right now, there's no body to be repatriated, is that right? That the only body we've come here for will be that of Samuel Dinsky, octogenarian, and still very much alive despite a nasty brain tumour which, if the specialists are right, should kill him within a few weeks?'

At the neighbouring tables, anxious faces had turned in their direction, which Ambroise ignored, continuing: 'You're very kind, but don't take me for a halfwit!'

'Have you ever heard of medically assisted suicide?' she calmly asked.

'Yes, as has everyone, sort of.'

'Well, that's the choice of an eighty-two-year-old man who refuses to allow death to toy with him once again as it did in the past. Those are his own words, Ambroise. Toy with him once again. He told me his whole story. Deported with his family when he was a child, Samuel lived through the horror of the concentration camps. Starvation, disease and death all around, stalking him, touching him, taking its victims but never choosing him. Imagine that kid barely twelve years old, whose job was to collect the spectacles of those taken to the gas chambers. Imagine for one second what he must have experienced, what he must have felt at the sight of those processions of human beings handing him their glasses, many of them unaware of the horror that lay in store for them.'

Ambroise recalled the image of Samuel dazed and weeping in front of the display of sunglasses at the motorway services. 'Some bad memories that caught up with me,' the old man had said, wiping away his tears.

'He doubted – and quite rightly, I think – that a firm such as yours would wittingly agree to be involved in a plan like this. And if he lied to you by inventing this twin brother, it was solely because for him it was the only way to achieve his purpose. His end, to be more precise. Have himself brought here, one of the few countries where medically assisted suicide is legal, catch death off guard and then be brought home. There, now you know as much as I do,' concluded Manelle, taking a large glug of wine.

'Shit,' said Ambroise for the second time that evening.

'It's an association called Deliverance that will take care of him. The director will be coming to the hotel tomorrow morning to take Samuel for the medical check-up. Then he'll take him to the apartment where, in the late afternoon, his . . .'

She shuddered and stopped herself from saying 'execution', which was on the tip of her tongue.

'He wants me to go with him, but . . .'

Manelle was unable to say any more and burst into tears. At that moment, Ambroise wanted more than ever to get up and hug her to him, stroke her hair and drink the pearls running down her cheeks. To say to her that he was there now, that he would be there tomorrow and all the tomorrows forever. Instead, glued to his chair by the stupid shyness that he despised, he merely handed her his napkin so she could dry her eyes.

'Thank you. I simply can't accept the idea. I keep telling myself we should let nature run its course. That in the midst of all the pain he's suffering, there might still be some happy moments to be had. And there's the possibility of a remission – there is such a thing, isn't there?'

'Are they certain about the tumour? Is there really nothing that can be done, no operation possible?'

'None. The consultant was categorical. It's cut-and-dried. His condition is deteriorating fast. This evening, he had a temperature again and it's becoming harder and harder to bring it down. Not to mention that he can barely keep any food down. And he told me earlier that his vision's blurred and he sometimes sees double.'

After a lengthy silence, Ambroise spoke again.

'I think we have to respect his choice, Manelle. Put

aside your own feelings and let Samuel depart in the way he has chosen. And if his last wish is to have you with him, then you have to support him. We'll do it together, if you like.'

Manelle remained silent. Silence as a way to avoid making a decision, she thought bitterly. But she knew deep down that Ambroise was right. And tomorrow, she and Ambroise would stay with Samuel Dinsky until he breathed his last.

When the waiter came back to take their order, they still hadn't looked at the menu. Ambroise had lost his appetite. More for form than because they were hungry, they both ordered sole meunière, the chef's speciality, and another glass of wine. At first, they ate gingerly, but gradually they perked up again, initially thanks to the tender fish fillet and crunchy chips, the wine's fruitiness, the laughter from the surrounding tables and the shimmering lights on the distant mountainsides. There was life in their eyes, in their pink cheeks. Then they talked, told each other about themselves, and caught themselves smiling and even laughing, putting aside for a moment the unbearable thought of the day that lay ahead.

32

By the time they left the restaurant, the mist over the lake had grown denser and was shrouding the opposite shore. Manelle was shivering with cold and Ambroise took off his jacket and put it around her shoulders. They walked quickly and were soon inside the hotel's heated lobby. When they entered the lift, Manelle snuggled up to Ambroise, resting her head on his shoulder.

'I don't want to be on my own tonight,' she entreated. 'Not tonight, please.'

Ambroise held her tight, breathed in the smell of her hair, giddy with her fragrance. They stood like that for a long time in the lift, outside time and outside the world. As soon as they were inside room 236, they kissed passionately. Their teeth knocked together as their tongues sought each other. Drunk on wine and desire, their heads were spinning. They wanted each other with every fibre of their beings. Still locked in a kiss, they undressed, separating only to remove their trousers. The bed greeted their bodies. Panting, Ambroise released Manelle's breasts from her bra. She tore off his boxers.

'Put the light on, please. I want to see you,' she asked him breathlessly.

The yellow glow from the wall lights chased the shadows, outlined their curves, made their eyes shine, and flooded the valley formed by their bellies pressed together. Manelle caressed his shoulders, kissed his chest. Ambroise cupped a breast in one of his hands while he slipped the other between her thighs. He shivered when she kissed his neck. She gasped as he caressed her, imprisoning his hand between her clenched legs.

'Come inside me,' she whispered in his ear as she nibbled it.

Ambroise entered her. Together they rode the storm of passion, until ecstasy submerged them and cast them adrift on the white sheets, side by side, panting and satiated for the time being.

33

They made love three times during the night, with the same hunger each time. Manelle stole back to room 103 at dawn. She didn't want Beth to worry on discovering her absence when she awoke. She put on a T-shirt and slid into the queen-sized bed next to Beth whose regular snores soon lulled her to sleep. At eight o'clock, reception telephoned the three rooms with their alarm call.

'Did you have a nice evening?' Beth asked Manelle in a mischievous tone. Between snores, she had not failed to notice the late hour at which Manelle had come to bed.

'Wonderful, yes. The fish was excellent and the lakeside is really beautiful.'

Beth didn't doubt for a moment that the 'wonderful' didn't only refer to the fish and the walk on the shore, but kept it to herself.

While Beth got dressed, Manelle went next door to see how Samuel was feeling. She kissed his forehead. He had a temperature again. Had it ever really subsided? she wondered. 'By this evening, it'll be better,' said Samuel wryly. She helped him into the bathroom and gave him some privacy while she unpacked his clothes from the suitcase. Pale green shirt, black trousers, dark green jacket. Green, the colour of hope, she thought. He meekly allowed himself to be dressed. He was as exhausted as the previous day, if not more so. Like the pills, nights no longer had any effect on him. Manelle asked him to lie down and have a rest while he waited for her.

'I'll be back in a minute,' she reassured him. 'I just need to have a shower and get dressed.'

Samuel was asleep by the time she came back. Seeing him lying still like that in the centre of his bed, in his clothes, his hands folded over his chest, she thought for a second that death, a bad loser, had preempted his plans. She stroked his cheek, smoothed with the back of her hand the rebel lock of hair which she always had to tame each time she visited him. He opened his eyes and looked at her without recognizing her. They were the eyes of a person lost in the middle of nowhere.

'It's me, Manelle,' she whispered tenderly. 'They're waiting for us downstairs for breakfast. You need sustenance, it's going to be a long day.'

Manelle bit her tongue, calling herself an idiot. How can a last day ever be long enough? They found Ambroise and his grandmother in the restaurant where a buffet breakfast awaited them. She greeted him with a light kiss.

'The secret of a good brioche dough is the same as that of a beautiful romance,' announced Beth, placing a plate of pastries on the table. 'A whole night for the dough to rise, which is what makes them so fluffy and light.'

Ambroise and Manelle exchanged a knowing look. Beth, who wasn't in the least surprised, tapped Samuel's hand and stood up to tie his napkin around his neck.

'It would be a sin to drop food on such a beautiful shirt.'

Manelle brought him a glass of orange juice. He

merely ate one madeleine which he pecked at reluctantly. Despite the palpable sadness, the two young people forced themselves to eat, unable to rid themselves of the unbearable thought that this shared breakfast was the old man's last.

'The person who is coming to fetch me to go and see my brother will be here at ten, won't they, Manelle?'

'He knows, Samuel,' she told him, placing her hand on his emaciated forearm. 'No need to lie any more, Ambroise knows, I told him everything last night.'

'That's right, Monsieur Dinsky,' confirmed Ambroise, 'Manelle told me everything.'

'Today, do please call me Samuel.'

'And I'd like to support you alongside Manelle, with your permission, Samuel.'

'Depart surrounded by two angels, I couldn't wish for more.'

'Beth,' continued Ambroise solemnly, turning to his grandmother. 'Samuel, Manelle and I have something to tell you.'

'If it's to talk to me about medically assisted suicide, don't waste your breath, Sammy has already told me everything.'

'When?'

'Yesterday, when we were at the picnic area, after

he'd vomited his guts out in the toilet and after I'd confessed I was your grandmother and not at all the volunteer he'd been led to believe I was. I didn't say anything because he asked me to keep quiet about it,' she went on, affectionately grasping Samuel's hand. 'He was afraid you'd turn around and drive back.'

Hmm, thought Ambroise, everyone except me seems to have a secret to hide.

The director of Deliverance walked into the lobby on the stroke of ten. Swiss precision timing, admired Beth. Emma Besuchet had a soft voice underscored by a strong Vaud accent. In her fifties, with a pleasant face and colourfully dressed, there was no hint of the austerity Manelle had expected about her, apart from her hair drawn back into a tight bun. Manelle wished she could hate this harbinger of death but wasn't able to find her disagreeable. She showed Samuel the utmost consideration and respect, and Manelle felt that her 'Good morning, Monsieur Dinsky' hit just the right note. After the introductions, Emma Besuchet invited them to adjourn to the secluded little hotel lounge with its armchairs and sofas. There, she explained the procedure to Samuel very clearly. She did so in her own words, using euphemisms that Ambroise knew all too well.

'The "departure" will take place in the early evening, at dusk, if you agree.'

Like thieves, thought Manelle, with a shudder.

'Of course, Monsieur Dinsky, you will remain in control of the situation throughout and you can choose to make any changes you wish. Let me remind you that Deliverance and I are there for the sole purpose of supporting you in your choice and to make it as humane and gentle as possible. At eleven o'clock we have an appointment with Doctor Meyan, the association's physician, who will check that your state of health complies with our code of ethics. A mere formality, don't worry. I'm going to ask you for your medical record.'

Manelle handed her the file with Samuel's medical history.

'Thank you. I also need a valid identity document.'

'I only have my identity card,' stuttered Samuel.

Manelle delicately took the wallet from his trembling hands and extracted the card, which she held out to Emma Besuchet. To everyone's great annoyance, the latter scrutinized the plastic rectangle for several long minutes.

'I see your card expired some months ago. Do you have any other form of ID? A passport or your birth certificate, for example, or, as long as it is no more than three months old, a recent extract from the civil status register? No? That's a nuisance. You really have nothing but this ID card?'

'For goodness' sake!' exclaimed Manelle, annoyed. 'You can see that it's definitely him.'

'I can see a document that expired last April. And that is the only thing that is valid legally. Over and above all humane considerations, which I understand perfectly well, we don't have the power or even less the right to determine a person's identity in a purely arbitrary manner.'

'For fuck's sake, you can see the condition he's in, can't you? What about his medical record, is that arbitrary?' fumed Manelle.

Emma Besuchet took Manelle to one side.

'Look, mademoiselle, there's no point making a scene. Losing your temper won't help us find a solution.'

'You can't do this to him. He has worked so hard to prepare himself,' pleaded Ambroise who had joined them.

'He can't stand the pain any more, dammit,' hissed Manelle. 'He vomits up everything he eats, can barely see and is as exhausted when he wakes up as he is when he goes to bed.'

Marooned on the large sofa, Samuel understood nothing of all the fuss. 'Is something the matter?' he asked Beth, who went over to sit next to him and took his hand.

'I don't know, but it seems there's a customs officer inside every Swiss person.'

'The regulations are very strict: you have to be able to prove you exist to request the right to die, it's as simple as that,' replied Emma Besuchet, before going over to Samuel.

She placed the ID card and medical file on the coffee table, apologizing profusely.

'I can only apologize, Monsieur Dinsky. This is the first time that such a thing has happened and please believe that I am deeply sorry, truly, but it is impossible for us to launch the process today. Naturally we will reimburse a percentage of the sum paid, having deducted our expenses. And we will of course remain entirely at your service should you wish to apply to us again, on condition that your documents are up to date. Goodbye, Monsieur Dinsky. Goodbye, mesdames, monsieur.'

Ambroise and Manelle stood rooted to the spot for

a moment, utterly defeated by the turn of events. Ambroise put his arms around Manelle.

'It's what you wanted deep down, isn't it?' he comforted her. 'That was even the reason you followed us to begin with, I believe. Come on, he needs us.'

Then, kneeling in front of him, taking one hand each, they explained to a distraught Samuel that he was not going to die that day, that he was going to have to endure his ordeal a while longer, but that they would be there beside him no matter what, as promised, to the end.

'Did he only see one specialist?' asked Beth, surprised, as she perused Samuel's medical record.

'Yes,' confirmed Manelle.

'Ambroise Larnier, what has your grandmother always taught you?'

'That specialists only see things with one eye. And that you should always seek a second opinion if you want the complete picture.'

34

'Can you remind us who your father is, Ambroise Larnier?' his grandmother asked him.

'What's that got to do with anything?' muttered Ambroise.

'Go on, answer, they'll find it of interest,' Beth insisted.

'Professor Henri Larnier, Nobel thingummy laureate, 2005,' muttered Ambroise contemptuously.

'Medicine, the Nobel Prize in Medicine. Let's not be afraid of saying it, if you please. And what is his specialism, this illustrious man, can you remind us?'

'Oh no, Beth, I can see where this is going, but it's out of the question. Not on your life.'

'Bravo, you couldn't find a more apt expression in the circumstances.'

'I apologize, Samuel, I didn't mean that, but don't ask me the impossible, Beth, not him.'

'What's all this about?' Manelle broke in.

'Well, the father of the young man standing before you happens to be one of the most eminent oncologists in the world, but this same young man, having fallen out with him, refuses to take advantage of this privilege to consult him.'

'But we must go there straight away, Ambroise,' exclaimed Manelle. 'We have nothing to lose. And we don't give a toss that you're not on speaking terms with your father, we're not asking you to patch things up with him, we just want him to see Samuel.'

'He's the leading expert in his field, Ambroise, as you well know,' urged Beth. 'What's more, luck is on our side. He should be in his office at the WHO, as he usually is at the beginning of the week. It's a stone's throw from here. Do it for Samuel.'

Samuel was staring at the floor, his eyes vacant, anticipating the departure he had just been refused. Ambroise swallowed his pride and gave in.

'OK, but don't expect me to grovel at his feet. It's purely for Samuel.'

'Thank you on his behalf,' gushed Manelle, kissing him on the lips and then gently taking Samuel's arm.

They drove along the lake shore in the direction of Geneva for some fifty kilometres. After around an hour, Ambroise drew up in front of the austere WHO headquarters. From the outside, the seven-storey building looked like a 1970s apartment complex. While Manelle stayed in the vehicle with Samuel – no point tiring him unnecessarily – Ambroise and his grandmother entered through the vast glass doors, went over to the reception desk and asked to see Professor Larnier.

'May I inquire who wishes to see him?' asked the receptionist.

'His son.'

'And his mother-in-law,' added Beth.

The woman gazed at them inquisitively and asked them to wait while she dialled a number.

'Professor Larnier is waiting for you in his office. Third floor, his name is on the door,' she said on hanging up.

They went to fetch Manelle and Samuel and the four of them stepped into the vast lift that whisked them up to the third floor. *PROFESSOR HENRI LARNIER, NOBEL PRIZE IN MEDICINE.* A door plate the size of the man's ego, thought Ambroise. They didn't need to knock. The door opened to reveal an alarmed Henri Larnier. The first thing that struck Ambroise at the sight of his father was that he had aged. A grey beard covered the lower part of his face. Now over sixty, he had lost a little of the stiff bearing that imbued his presence with authority. A rather handsome man, thought Manelle, and whose son looks very much like him, even though Ambroise had a laid-back manner that was cruelly lacking in his father.

'What's going on?' asked the professor anxiously, before even greeting his son.

'Hello, Father,' chided Ambroise.

'I'm sorry. Hello, Ambroise. Hello, Elisabeth.'

Countless times his mother-in-law had asked him to call her Beth, but in vain. Calling things and people by their precise names was typical of his father's scientific nature, Ambroise said to himself. In life as in medicine, you didn't mess with names.

'Sir, young lady.'

'Manelle and Samuel,' Ambroise introduced them.

'To what do I owe the pleasure of this visit?'

'Don't worry, I'm not here on my own account.'

'You don't come and see me when I'm close to you, so you must appreciate that I find your presence here, hundreds of kilometres from home, accompanied by your grandmother and these two strangers, somewhat intriguing.'

'Could we come into your office, if you don't mind?'

'There aren't enough chairs. I suggest we go down to the cafeteria instead, we can talk more comfortably there,' suggested Henri Larnier, closing the door behind him.

On neutral ground, thought his son wryly. His father had never been able to let him into his world. They found a free table and Henri Larnier repeated his question.

'So, to what do I owe this visit?'

'Well, I'd like . . . we'd like you to examine this gentleman and read his medical record to find out exactly what is wrong with him.'

'So, my son is interested in the living these days,' replied Henri Larnier snidely.

'Please, Henri,' entreated Beth, 'Ambroise has taken it upon himself to come and make this request. Don't quarrel now, I beg you.'

'It was bound to happen,' grumbled Ambroise.

'Oh no,' protested Manelle, 'you're not going to start. I don't know what the problem is between you, and it's none of my business, but that's not what matters right now. What matters, Professor Larnier, is the tumour that's killing our friend here, so you can resume your argument later, but meanwhile, take care of him, please!' commanded Manelle, plonking Samuel's medical file down in front of the flabbergasted doctor.

'Very well,' he conceded, opening the file.

Henri Larnier ignored his colleague's report and skimmed the results of the tests, then scrutinized the MRI images for what felt like an eternity, without saying a word.

'From the date, I see these images were taken around two months ago, is that correct?'

Manelle answered on Samuel's behalf.

'Just under two months, yes.'

'Just under two months,' he repeated dubiously. 'Not possible,' he muttered to himself.

'What isn't possible?' asked Beth.

'Forgive my candour, but given the size of the glioblastoma at the time the MRI was done, and knowing the rapid invasive power and very aggressive nature of this type of tumour, it is scientifically impossible that the gentleman here present should still be alive. I'm sorry but no, quite simply scientifically impossible. I don't know what to think, Monsieur . . . Wendling,' he went on, reading the name at the bottom of the images, 'but—'

'Dinsky,' chorused Manelle, Beth and Ambroise.

'I'm sorry?'

'Dinsky. Not Wendling but Dinsky,' Manelle corrected him.

'Look, it says Wendling here, Roger Wendling,' insisted Henri Larnier, showing them the name written in white letters on a black background at the bottom of the scans.

There was stupefaction on all their faces except on that of Samuel, who was too preoccupied with battling his headache. Henri Larnier put the image down and picked up the file again.

'I see that the report written by my colleague, Doctor . . . Gervaise, is about Monsieur Dinsky but it is based on the scans labelled Wendling. Very generous, this Doctor Gervaise. To give three months' life expectancy to a patient suffering from a glio like that, bravo, that's not optimism, it's science fiction. There must have been a mix-up, something which occurs less and less frequently, thank goodness, but it does some-times still happen.'

'So what is wrong with Monsieur Dinsky, then?' asked Beth, with a mixture of anxiety and hope.

'To find out, we'll have to do more tests. How old are you, Monsieur Dinsky?'

'Eighty-two,' replied Samuel weakly.

'And you were experiencing recurrent migraines, which is why you went to see the specialist, is that correct?'

'Yes,' replied Manelle, speaking for Samuel.

'Fever?'

'Yes, almost all the time over the past few days.'

'Vomiting? Weight loss?'

'Yes, he vomits almost everything he eats and he has grown very thin.'

'Does he complain about his eyesight? Blurred or double vision?'

'Yes, he has been complaining recently, but how do you know?'

Henri Larnier rose and went over to Samuel. He felt his temples and examined his temporal arteries, which were abnormally swollen.

'If I touch your scalp here, does it hurt?'

'Yes,' groaned Samuel.

'Have you ever heard of Horton's disease?'

The question was addressed to all of them. The ensuing silence invited him to continue: 'It is a disease that chiefly occurs in the elderly, generally over the age of eighty, and which displays the symptoms we've just mentioned. If it isn't treated rapidly, the most serious risk is the deterioration of the eyesight, sometimes resulting in total blindness. But don't worry, it is a disease that is easily treatable nowadays. I'm going to prescribe Monsieur Dinsky an emergency treatment based on powerful corticosteroids and if it is indeed Horton's disease – which the tests will confirm very quickly – his general condition should improve rapidly and the headaches cease within a few days, a few hours even.'

Ambroise, Beth and Manelle all stared at Samuel Dinsky, a Samuel Dinsky who was utterly befuddled and whose world, for the second time that day, had just been turned upside down.

35

The man of science had Samuel do a blood test at the WHO laboratories. The results would come through that afternoon. At the same time, he wrote out a prescription for the pharmacy in the basement so that the corticosteroid treatment could begin as soon as possible.

'There you are. You can collect the medication from reception in a few minutes with the dosage to be followed to the letter and a note for the GP. Take the first dose right away, there's no time to lose. Goodness, it's been ages since we have practised like this,' beamed a smug Henri Larnier. 'It's a bit chaotic,

I admit, but it reminds me of my years as a junior doctor.'

For the first time, Ambroise detected nostalgia in his father's voice, nostalgia perhaps for the time before the Nobel laureate had replaced the doctor.

'I must leave you,' he went on, glancing at his watch, 'I have a lecture to prepare, but you are welcome to stay here for lunch if you wish. The canteen food is good, you'll see. And I don't know what to do with all the luncheon vouchers I'm entitled to every month.'

Henri Larnier put the vouchers down on the table and gave Samuel a few words of reassurance.

'If we are correct, Monsieur Dinsky, everything should soon be back to normal, don't worry.'

Ambroise smiled. He had forgotten his father's strange habit of using the royal 'we' when he spoke of himself, a habit that came from his countless scientific publications in which it is standard to use the first-person plural.

Once he'd left, Manelle and Ambroise looked into each other's eyes, which held a fresh glimmer of hope. Emma Besuchet and her goodbye cocktail were far away. Samuel was going to live. Today, which was to have been his last, was going to be a new birth. Beth, with her usual practical nature, brought everyone back down to earth.

'We'd better go and have something to eat before it gets too busy. It's midday and people are beginning to arrive.'

'Go on,' commanded Ambroise. 'Have what you like. I'm going to reception to see if the medication is there.'

Ambroise returned clutching the bag containing the precious packets of corticosteroids to his chest. In accordance with the dose prescribed by Henri Larnier, Manelle took out three pills which she set down in front of Samuel. Laboriously, he swallowed the pills one at a time with a glass of water, urged on by his guardian angels. Guardian angels who ate quickly and with appetite, released from the weight that had been burdening them since the morning. When it was time to leave, Ambroise gave Manelle the keys and excused himself.

'Wait for me in the car. I'll be out in five minutes.'

He ignored the lift and raced up the stairs to the third floor. He hadn't thanked his father for having devoted a little of his precious time to them. Most of all, he wanted to embrace him, the way a son should embrace his father when they part. His timid knocks went unanswered. 'Papa?' He went in. The office was deserted. Then he saw. And the minute he discovered Henri Larnier's lair, all the stupid certainties about the great man that he'd cultivated over the years – egocentrism, pride, coldness, lack of sensitivity – were annihilated, swept away by the sight that met his eyes. Everywhere around him, hanging on the walls, displayed on the bookshelves, standing on the mahogany desk, were photos of Ambroise and his mother. Ambroise as a baby in Cécile's arms, Ambroise as a child playing with a stethoscope, his mother in a swimsuit posing by the pool, radiant in the sunshine, Ambroise as a teenager, playing the guitar, Ambroise by the Christmas tree unwrapping his presents, Cécile with Ambroise on her knees, deciphering his first words, Ambroise in his father's white coat, way too big for him, Cécile absorbed in reading Louis-Ferdinand Céline's *Journey to the End of the Night*. A sanctuary – Henri Larnier's office was a sanctuary dedicated to his ghosts, that of the wife he had loved and of the son who had escaped him. Ambroise raised his hand to his mouth on discovering the bookcase. Not for a moment would he have imagined that his father might be interested in his work. But there, carefully arranged on the centre shelf, were several books on the art of embalming and the profession of embalmer. Books including some recent works on the latest innovations. Shaken, Ambroise wrote his mobile phone number on a piece of paper which he placed on the blotter, inviting his father to call him as soon as he had the results of the tests. Then he added at the bottom of the note those words that were never said, words that remained trapped at the back of his throat out of embarrassment, words that sometimes find expression on the base of a funeral bier when it's too late, words which were worth a thousand embraces: *Your loving son*.

36

That Wednesday morning, sprawled in his vast hotel bed, Samuel Dinsky woke up amazed. Something had jolted him awake, something he hadn't experienced for ages: hunger. His empty stomach was gurgling with discontent and his taste buds were crying out for breakfast. The vice which, still the previous day, had been compressing his head, had now completely relaxed its grip, and the pain had evaporated. Now his head was breathing, as if there were a light breeze behind his frontal bone which had blown the last vestiges of pain far away. He got up and half opened the curtains. The ray of light that broke through and landed on the bed did not bring with it the millions of needles that usually pierced his retinas. No, he only felt the normal dazzle of daylight entering after a night spent in the dark. Samuel stretched, giving a contented moan as he lay in the sun, letting his body soak up the warmth. Only then did he see them. Manelle, Beth and Ambroise, standing at the foot of the bed, greeting him with a chorus of, 'Well?'

Back from Geneva, Samuel, dropping with exhaustion, had gone to bed and fallen asleep at once. 'The day turned out to be longer than planned,' he'd joked before falling asleep. Manelle, Ambroise and Beth had stayed with him, more vigilant than ever. Death, deprived of this long-promised prey, perhaps hadn't had its final say. Samuel had sweated out his fever through every pore of his skin and Manelle, assisted by Ambroise, had had to change his pyjamas for a dry T-shirt. Despite their insistence that she should go and rest in her room, Beth had refused point-blank. 'It's not every day you have the opportunity to watch over an eighty-two-year-old newborn,' she had whispered with the utmost seriousness. And so they had all kept a vigil at Samuel's bedside in room 101, watching over him in the dark, listening to his breathing, alert for the slightest wobble, until sleep overcame them too in the dead of night, Manelle in the armchair, Beth on the sofa and Ambroise on the floor where he had eventually lain down.

Samuel gazed at the trio staring at him on tenterhooks, waiting for his reply. The huge smile that lit up his face said more than any words could.

'What about your fever?' inquired Manelle, going over to give him a kiss.

His forehead was warm and dry.

'D-day plus one, Monsieur Samuel Dinsky. The first day of the rest of your life,' announced Ambroise solemnly, referring to the film by Rémi Bezançon.

The previous day, at the very same hour when he should have been drinking his lethal potion, Manelle had woken Samuel to give him his second dose of corticosteroids. And that morning, instead of lying on a stainless-steel table, waiting for the embalmer in the chill of death, he was before them, outstretched among the bedclothes, basking in the sunlight, more alive than ever. An eighty-two-year-old newborn. Beth could not have put it better. Alive thanks to an out-of-date ID card, thought Ambroise, horrified. And to the farsightedness of his father who had called him later that afternoon to confirm that it was indeed a case of Horton's disease.

'Will you come and visit me at home?' Henri Larnier had asked.

There had been a hint of anxiety in his voice. Fear that his son might say no, perhaps. Fear that the words written on the scrap of paper left on the blotter and which he'd read and reread then carefully put away in his wallet were empty words. *Your loving son.*

'I promise we'll come over, Papa. At least once a month, if only to renew Monsieur Dinsky's prescription, now that you're his doctor,' Ambroise had joked.

Henri Larnier's laugh was music to his ears.

D-day plus one for us too, Papa, thought Ambroise. Manelle had a breakfast tray brought up for Samuel. He wolfed down a piece of bread and butter, watched affectionately by Beth who hastily buttered another slice for him.

37

That evening, Samuel insisted on inviting them to dinner in the Regent's restaurant. 'To celebrate my Norton's disease', was his excuse.

'Horton, Sammy,' Beth corrected him. 'It's Horton.'

'I would never have imagined that one day I could be so overjoyed at having an illness,' confessed the octogenarian.

Samuel had put on his smart green suit for the occasion. 'It's the only one I have,' he apologized to Beth. 'And besides, no one will know that it's my death suit,' he added as they made their way down to the lobby. Meanwhile, Beth had had no hesitation either in donning her mourning outfit, without the veil. 'Black is suitable for any occasion,' she informed her grandson before he could open his mouth. 'Isn't that so, Manelle?'

'You both look magnificent,' Manelle congratulated them.

The centre table awaited them. 'I've always dreamed of one day dining ensconced in a Voltaire armchair surrounded by an army of waiters ready to pander to my every wish, and now my dream has come true,' said Manelle, darting Ambroise a mischievous look as they sat down. They joked throughout the meal, sometimes laughing heartily in the sedate atmosphere of the restaurant, under the incredulous stares of the other guests. Beth, behaving like a dowager, relished having so many waiters dancing attendance on her and summoned them to satisfy her every whim.

'May I have a glass of still water, my good man?'

'Would it be possible to have a slice of wholemeal bread? White bread gives me heartburn, thank you.'

'Would you be so kind as to bring me a warm, wet towel to wipe my hands?'

'Beth, that's going a bit far,' Ambroise chided her.

'What? Having all these waiters at one's beck and call and not being allowed to make use of them would be as stupid as putting candles on a birthday cake and not being permitted to light them.'

On leaving the table, Beth shelled out a generous tip of ten euros.

'They don't want to be part of Europe but they'll have my euros all the same,' she trumpeted victoriously.

Manelle went to tuck Samuel up in bed while Ambroise gave Beth her injection.

'You each have your own old person, fair's fair,' she joked. 'You know, darling, I wouldn't want to hold you back,' she went on with the utmost seriousness. 'If one day you want to move out and live your own life, you mustn't feel you have to stay because of me.'

'Really? Can I? And I was staying because I thought you couldn't do without me. Yes, but on the other hand, I can't leave you all alone, with your diabetes and everything. No, we're going to have to find you a nice little old people's home. I know one that's not too expensive where you'll be able to make lots of nice friends, attend cake-baking workshops, play cards and join the reading group. I'll come and see you on Sundays and we'll go for a walk in the grounds. It'll be lovely.'

At the sight of his grandmother's crestfallen look,

Ambroise hurriedly reassured her, and hugged her tight.

'Don't be silly, I'm joking. You know very well that I could never live without your cakes! But tonight, I'm afraid I'm going to have to deprive you of your young roommate,' he added, grabbing Manelle round the waist as she came over to join them.

'Make the most of it, you lovebirds. Oh, yes, make the most of it. Love's like sweets, there's no point just looking at them,' she retorted with a stage wink.

38

The next day, when they were both standing at the breakfast buffet, Beth-the-Busybody couldn't help asking Manelle if they'd slept well.

'We ate sweets all night,' Manelle whispered.

'Wonderful! Make sure there are always some left in the packet,' advised Beth-the-Wise.

They'd agreed to leave at ten o'clock sharp, and they met in reception with their luggage. Samuel paid the bill and cancelled the reservations for the remaining nights.

'Stay cut short, life extended!' Beth gleefully

informed the receptionist, who nodded politely without even trying to understand.

The mood was cheerful on the return journey. They drove along the lake shore one last time. An ancient paddle-steamer was sailing on the silvery waters, its two wheels churning up an effervescent froth. The red flag with its white cross attached to the stern flapped in the wind. Craning forward like a child, Samuel missed nothing of the landscape flying past. When they reached the border, in answer to the customs officer who asked if they had anything to declare, Beth said, 'Only a life.' Seeing the smiles of the other occupants, the official didn't press the matter and wondered how people could be so cheerful in such a sinister vehicle as he watched the hearse leave Switzerland. They spoke little, communing in silence with mere looks. They were happy. They had come with death as the fifth passenger and were leaving without it. Four souls who had never felt so alive.

39

Bouba and Abel greeted Ambroise with their customary good humour, in their office festooned with Christmas decorations. The fragile branches of the *ficus* were bowed under an avalanche of tinsel. From the ceiling hung countless coloured glass balls. An army of crib figures had invaded the top of the fridge. Sellotaped to the door, jolly, paunchy Santas welcomed visitors with their merry smiles. A few days away from Christmas, the two stooges did not seem to want to take off the red hats rammed down on their heads from morning to night. As he often did, the tall

Boubacar replied to Ambroise's greeting with one of his jokes.

'Have you heard the one about the skeleton who goes into a cafe? The waiter asks him what he wants to drink, and the skeleton replies, "A beer . . . and a floor cloth, please."'

Abel waited for Bouba to stop laughing before opening his mouth.

'Have you come to see the little lady? I don't understand why they go to the trouble of doing autopsies on the over-nineties. Can't they leave them in peace?'

'You know very well that it's obligatory in the case of a fire, especially in a retirement home,' replied Ambroise.

'The fire was caused by Christmas lights in one of the ground-floor rooms, apparently,' said Bouba.

'I don't know. I only hope she didn't suffer. Where is she?'

'She's still on the autopsy table. We thought it would make your job easier. Just transfer her to the trolley when you've finished and we'll take her up to the chapel of rest. Take your time, there's no family,' added Abel.

'If I dared, I'd even say the heat's off!' chortled Bouba.

Ambroise thought he'd misunderstood.

'What do you mean, no family? It is Madame de Morbieux you're talking about?'

'Mademoiselle de Morbieux, if you please. No, no family, that's what the manager of the home told us.'

As the lift took him down to level -2, Ambroise hastily called Le Clos de la Roselière. After introducing himself, he asked for confirmation. The girl who answered was in tears.

'It's so dreadful, Monsieur Larnier. Just think, three dead. Three! No, Isabelle had no family. Some distant great-nephews but they never came to see her. You were her only visitor, every year on her birthday. Oh, how she used to talk about her embalmer. She was very fond of you, you know. The days following your visit, she would sing your praises non-stop.'

'She told me her husband had died a long time ago but she would often talk to me about her daughter who used to take her out for lunch every Sunday.'

'Pure make-believe, Monsieur Larnier. She was never married and she certainly had no children. Isabelle was a gifted storyteller. That was her profession, she was a writer.'

'But what about her grandchildren and great-grandchildren who made drawings for her. I didn't dream them up, all those drawings tacked to the walls of her room.'

'Oh, those drawings were done by the pupils at the local primary school for the residents of the home. You'll find some in all the rooms. No, I'm sorry Monsieur Larnier. In a way, we and you were her only family.'

Isabelle de Morbieux's naked body awaited Ambroise on the stainless-steel table. The pathologist had confirmed the cause of death as asphyxiation. Ambroise put down his cases and went over to the body. Like the other two victims of the fire that had ravaged the east wing of Le Clos de la Roselière, the nonagenarian had been asleep in her bed and had been suffocated by the smoke. The flames hadn't had time to reach her body and her face had remained intact in death. After an autopsy, the embalming process was always time-consuming and delicate. While he washed the body with a damp cloth, the old lady's vibrant voice echoed in his ears, as clearly as when it had rung out in the Orchid room. 'Tell me about you, Ambroise. You never talk to me about yourself.' Ambroise smiled. Then, as his hands ran over the white, mottled flesh, he started to talk. He told her about Manelle, her indignant shrieks and her dumbfounded look when they had first met. Manelle and her fiery eyes. Manelle and her jet-black hair, lithe body and intoxicating smell, and her precious laugh. Manelle and her lips which he could never have enough of. He explained how they both spent their days counting the hours until they could be together again in the evenings.

'The Jeandrons moved out of their apartment on the second floor last month. We leapt at the opportunity. I only have to go up one floor to give Beth her jab. Oh, Beth, I haven't told you about Beth, Isabelle. I know you'd have loved her.'

Ambroise carried on talking while he went about the embalming process. Soon the hum of the injection pump mingled with his words.

'You should have seen Odile Chambon's dismay when we took the mog back on our return from Morges. She was so upset, Beth offered to share the cat with her. And that's what they've been doing for the past three months. Alternate weeks, one week of *fars bretons* on the third floor, one week of endless cuddles and caressing on the ground floor. The tom doesn't seem to mind, he seems to be perfectly happy with his two mistresses. Oh yes, and the theatre has started up again. Did I tell you I was involved with a theatre company? We've taken on a new recruit in the shape of Beth. We needed an actress to play an elderly lady. You should see her standing in the spotlight, performing her part. The entire company has fallen in love with her, despite her unfortunate habit of always changing the lines to suit herself.'

Talking all the while, Ambroise manipulated the body. He sometimes broke off while he inserted a cannula or sutured an orifice, then he picked up where he had left off. He spoke to her at length about Samuel and how the old man delighted in every new day on this earth.

'He and Manelle took the MRI scans back to Doctor Gervaise. He pulled a strange face, the specialist did, when Samuel pitched up in his consulting room in tip-top shape. He looked as if he'd seen a ghost, Manelle told me.'

Talking non-stop, Ambroise proceeded to dress the body. He eased Isabelle de Morbieux's favourite floral dress over her satin slip, knotted the silk scarf around her neck, and adorned her white hair with a slide. He lightly made up her face and spritzed her cheeks with eau de Cologne. Ambroise always carried some with him; it was useful for masking the smell of the embalming products. 'Eau de Cologne, I've never worn any other perfume,' the old lady had told him on each of his visits. 'My husband used to love it.'

'Isabelle de Morbieux, you're one hell of a liar,' Ambroise admonished her with a smile. 'In three days, it'll be Christmas,' he went on. 'We're all going to my father's. Since we've been back from Morges, we phone each other every Sunday and I drop in to see him from time to time. We tell each other what we've been up to, me my cadavers and him his seminars. We often talk about Mother. She has come back to us, her memories have filled the gulf that lay between us. Papa insisted on inviting us. Even Samuel will be coming too. And I won't be surprised if the Yule log is a Black Forest gateau this year.'

Ambroise leaned over the deceased to whisper in her ear.

'Christmas Day, the nativity. A good day to tell everyone that there's a little baby in Manelle's tummy, don't you think, Isabelle?'

The old woman's voice rang in his mind, clear and joyful: 'A hell of a good day, Ambroise!'

40

For some time now, it had seemed to Marcel Mauvinier that his home help's attitude had changed. The state of permanent exasperation that had previously pushed Manelle Flandin to the brink of rebellion and delighted the old man had given way to a worrying serenity. She carried out all the chores listed on the sheet of squared paper willingly. He was suspicious, wondering what this apparent tranquillity boded. This morning, there was something else not quite right but he couldn't put his finger on it. At first, the young woman's behaviour had seemed no different from usual. As was her habit, she had slammed the door when she came in and yelled from the passage 'It's only me' loud enough to wake the dead, had come to say good morning to him in the sitting room as she did five times a week, skimmed the instructions waiting for her on the kitchen table then gone to empty the enamel chamber pot down the toilet and rinse it thoroughly. But something wasn't right, Marcel Mauvinier was convinced. The feeling was as irritating as a stone in his shoe, arousing in him a nagging sense of unease. He closed the newspaper and fidgeted in his chair. Never had it felt so uncomfortable. Should he see this disquiet as a grim foreboding? He ended up persuaded that Mademoiselle Flandin, home help by profession and a blatant thief, like all of them – of that he was convinced and would soon prove – had decided that morning to act and fleece the inoffensive old man that he was of his fifty-euro note. Merely thinking about the theft only increased the old man's vigilance and he did not take his eyes off the TV screen that served as a monitor.

Today, he'd hidden the note inside the microwave on the kitchen counter, certain that even the most cunning mice eventually give in to temptation. Through the dark glass, you could guess at rather than see the bill lying in the centre of the turntable. After tidying the bedroom, putting on a wash and sweeping the passage, Manelle reappeared in the kitchen, humming to herself. She who sings last will sing longest, thought the old man. Using the remote lying on his knee, he switched to camera three. The old man saw his home help start to 'clean coffee maker' next to the microwave, as instructed in his cramped handwriting between 'sweep the passage' and 'empty dishwasher'. At first, he thought the trick wasn't going to work, that she would clean the percolator without even glancing at the oven, but the unmistakeable sound of the microwave door opening make his heart leap. She'd found the note! His eyes glued to his screen, Marcel Mauvinier watched every single one of Manelle's movements. For a few seconds, she turned away from him, offering only the sight of her back. Then, what he had so long been hoping for happened. He fathomed rather than saw her hand thrust rapidly into the pocket of her overall and then heard the microwave door bang sharply shut. The sound of a trap snapping on its prey, he thought, jubilant. As she emptied the dishwasher, Manelle sang. In a soft voice full of warmth, which the old man had never heard before, she was singing 'Who's afraid of the big bad wolf' as she whizzed around the kitchen clattering pots and pans. Even more than her choice of the Disney song, the way his home help had of looking defiantly at the camera between refrains alarmed him. All this stank. It was not good at all. But he'd got her. The video images would be self-evident, her kleptomaniac tendency would be unmasked and she'd have to explain herself to her employer.

That morning, Marcel Mauvinier didn't bother to check his watch to ensure that the forty-eight minutes paid for by the agency were up. Manelle was barely out of the door when he padded into the kitchen and flung open the oven door. The old man gazed at the dark mouth of the microwave, gobsmacked. The fifty-euro note numbered U18190763573 had disappeared. In its place, lying flat on the glass tray, was another note which he snatched with trembling hands and turned over every which way. He sniffed it, felt it and held it up to the light. The newly minted bill's denomination was printed above the baroque arch. The image danced in front of his eyes. One hundred euros. One hundred euros that scorched the flesh of his fingers. He put the note back where he had found it. His mind was seething. The question banged around inside his head. Why had the minx done that? It suddenly dawned on him that he couldn't spend that money. The note didn't fully belong to him, it belonged to both of them. Fifty-fifty. Marcel Mauvin-ier swore. The young home help had caught him in his own trap. It finally dawned on him what it was that had been making him feel uneasy but that he hadn't been able to put his finger on: that morning, when she came to say hello, Manelle Flandin had smiled at him for the first time.

ACKNOWLEDGEMENTS

I couldn't have concluded this book without thanking my friend Jules Rizet who very kindly opened the doors of the mysterious universe of embalming to me. I am grateful to him for allowing me to witness this practice that is both intense and full of humanity. It is a testimony to his respect for the deceased, his humility when confronted with the challenges of his profession, his immense expertise and sincere empathy towards the bereaved. He has his own very special way of putting his love for the living into his service of the dead. I will always be indebted to him for this experience, from which I returned more alive than ever.